Her
DESTINY

Her
DESTINY

ALANA PULLEN

HER DESTINY

iUniverse books may be ordered through booksellers or by contacting:

iUniverse
1663 Liberty Drive
Bloomington, IN 47403
www.iuniverse.com
1-800-Authors (1-800-288-4677)

Because of the dynamic nature of the Internet, any web addresses or links contained in this book may have changed since publication and may no longer be valid. The views expressed in this work are solely those of the author and do not necessarily reflect the views of the publisher, and the publisher hereby disclaims any responsibility for them.

Any people depicted in stock imagery provided by Thinkstock are models, and such images are being used for illustrative purposes only. Certain stock imagery © Thinkstock.

ISBN: 978-1-5320-4070-2 (sc)
ISBN: 978-1-5320-4071-9 (e)

Library of Congress Control Number: 2018900559

Print information available on the last page.

iUniverse rev. date: 01/16/2018

CHAPTER 1

IT WAS FINALLY GOING TO be the big day tomorrow; Sadie was moving to her new beach apartment in San Diego and starting her college life with her best friend. Ever since she was a little girl, it had always been her dream to live by the beach and enjoy the fun, sun, and surf. Now it was finally happening, and she was beyond excited to be able to see the ocean every day. It would practically be in her backyard from now on, and she could finally say goodbye to the hot desert that she had lived in all her life.

Yuma wasn't a bad place to live; it just wasn't what she wanted for herself and San Diego could offer her so much more. There was a swarm of butterflies of pure excitement and fear flying around in her stomach that she couldn't get a grip on so, for her last night at home, she went out to her favorite tree behind the house and sat under the stars to calm her nerves and say goodbye to her old life and accept her new life.

"Sadie?"

She couldn't help but hang her head in defeat, not

evening getting ten minutes alone before her older sister was already on her again. She knew Laura was trying to help, but this was her favorite spot, and it was the only time she could get true peace and quiet, which meant no visitors.

"There you are. Didn't you hear me calling you? Honestly, why you are out here? Is it because you're having a hard time leaving for college tomorrow?" Laura asked while taking a seat next to Sadie.

She didn't want to answer 101 questions, so it was time for the glare. Maybe Laura would get the message but when Sadie looked up and saw the concern and worry in her big sister's eyes, all her defenses easily broke down. She loved her older sister too much to fight with her or lie to her the night before she left. Laura and her husband, Luke, had been there for her, her whole life, so she figured she should at least admit the truth before leaving them behind.

"Maybe," she whispered as she turned her eyes back up to the stars, hoping the answers were up there somehow.

Sadie had always found the night sky to be beautiful. It always calmed her in a way because it felt like the stars were looking down at her and telling her that they were with her and she wasn't alone. It almost felt like they understood her better than anyone else did.

"I know it's a huge deal moving away from home for the first time," Laura said. "It can be really scary—it was for me too—so if you have doubts, I'd completely get it. I'm here to talk if you need me."

"That's not it," Sadie told her sister. "I want to go. It's

been my dream to live by the beach ever since we had our summer vacations with Mom and Dad there every year."

Sadie smiled as the memories came back to her in a flood—all the sandcastles that she and Dad had built and the seashell-hunting contests that she, Mom, and Laura would go on and even now she still had every seashell in her room in a blue glass bottle on her dresser.

"Yeah, I loved those trips too. But then what's the problem? Why are you out here all alone and looking like you lost your favorite toy?"

"It's just that I don't want to make the same mistake twice. I want to make friends for once and enjoy my life instead of always being scared of people finding out about my gift. I'm just tired of always hiding."

"I know it was hard for you, and I'm sorry about that but you've known this is our family gift and Mom would've wanted us to take care of it and help as many people as we can, just like she did."

She had to bite her tongue when Laura said the word *hard*. It wasn't even remotely close to hard. It would have been more accurate to say it was completely unbearable. This supposed gift had felt more like a curse to her than anything else. She figured Laura must have forgotten about the past, but to her she hadn't. There were simply too many bad experiences to count, and it had all started when she was walking down the hall in middle school like any other student and in just one moment, everything fell apart, and her life became a nightmare after that. In truth, she hadn't helped anybody, because all she wanted was to be left alone.

"I get that this gift was important to Mom, but it took

everything from me, You have no idea how alone I feel because of that. When I finally learned how to control this gift and protect myself so I could at least try to be around normal people, it was already too late, I had lost too much so excuse me if I'm a little bitter about that."

In truth if She had one wish, it would be that their parents were there with them. Mom always had the right words to say to make Sadie feel better when she was younger. One of her mom's favorites quotes was "You won't know if you can't do something unless you go out and try. If you fail, just get up and try again because nothing is impossible if you're determined enough."

Sadie and Laura's mom had been a great person. It would have been perfect to have her there in that moment to help her prepare for a new chapter of her life with no fear. Sadly, their parents had died unexpectedly when she was twelve and Laura was twenty, and since then, she had carried a huge pain in her heart every time she thought of them. She did love her sister and was beyond grateful to have her in her life, but it still felt like half of her soul was missing with their parents being gone and even all those years later, she still often asked herself why everything had fallen apart that night.

"Come on. Let's head in," Laura said as she stood up and dusted off her pants. "It's getting kind of late. Besides, you will feel better in the morning after a good night's rest."

She realized her sister was probably right. She could feel her eyes becoming heavy with fatigue from packing all day, and some rest would help clear her head a bit and maybe get rid of some of her crazy fears.

"Is Luke coming with us?" Sadie asked.

"Yeah, he took the day off to drive us up there."

Luke and Laura had met during their senior year of high school and had been together ever since. When they graduated from college, the first thing they did was get married and Luke went on to build his own construction company, while Laura became an ER nurse.

Sadie always felt the reason her sister decided to be a nurse had a lot to do with their parents' sudden deaths. Laura wanted to try to stop that pain and the sadness they felt from happening to anybody else if she could. Sadie was so proud and amazed by the strength of her sister's spirit. She wished at times that the family gift had been passed on to Laura instead because her sister would have handled the responsibility a lot better than she had and their mom would have been so proud probably.

"Hey, honey, is everything ready to go for tomorrow?" Laura called out to Luke, who was bent over the engine compartment of the SUV.

The second Luke heard Laura's voice, he looked up at her with a smile on his face and then started walking toward her while wiping his hands on a rag.

Luke had coal-black hair and emerald-green eyes. He was about six two and muscular, but that would be expected from working construction all his life. He now owned his own business and even now, Luke had never been an office guy, and so he was always working right along with his men at every job site.

Laura and Sadie looked very similar. They both had blonde hair, although Laura's ended at her shoulders, while Sadie's continued down her back and ended just at the top of her butt. Laura had light-brown eyes, while Sadie had hazel. Sadie was taller than Laura by a couple of inches and slightly heavier, but that was to be expected with Laura's busy work schedule and plus, Laura worked out every day on the treadmill. There was no way for Sadie to catch up to how fit her sister was, and besides, she told Sadie that it helped to stay in shape for her job so she could help as many people as possible without wasting a moment.

"Yeah," Luke answered Laura. "Just got done with the final tune-up, so we should be good to go tomorrow." He then leaned down and gave Laura a kiss on the lips.

It was easy to see the love between them was strong and unbreakable, plus, it was so romantic. Sadie hoped to find a love like that someday.

"What time is Jace coming by in the morning?" Laura asked while leaning her head on Luke's shoulder.

Jace was Sadie's best friend and her new roommate starting tomorrow. They had met during middle school when it was far too painful for Sadie to be around people, so she did her best to avoid people in order to keep herself safe. That all changed when a boy with dark-brown hair and rich, chocolate eyes came up to her one day in the school and said, "Hey, I'm Jace. What's your name?"

At first, Sadie avoided Jace and would walk away from him without another word; however, that didn't stop him from showing up every day and introducing himself. She started to notice that somehow this boy seemed different to her, but there was still a big part of her that didn't want to say anything to him and wanted him to go away. Then one day she decided to take the gamble and ended up telling him her name. The weirdest thing was that after telling him her name, she almost felt happy—like she was at peace, and all the pain and anger that had consumed her seemed to fade away. All she could think about was how she wanted to be close to this boy as much as possible. They had since become the best of friends and were as close as two people could get.

Her mind wandered back to the question Laura had asked. "When I talk to him earlier, he said that he'd be here at six," she answered.

"Good. That gives us plenty of time to be on the road by seven," Luke said.

"Yeah, well I'm heading to bed now, so I'll see you guys in the morning," Sadie said.

"Night, Sadie. See you in the morning," Laura called out to her.

She wave at her sister and Luke one more time before walking through the front door and shutting it behind her. As she was closing her bedroom door, she heard a familiar voice.

"Hey, babe,"

It was Jace. Sadie couldn't help but smile. "Hey yourself, are you all packed up?" she asked as she went and sat next to him on the bed.

"Yeah, but I know my girl, and I knew right now she would be worrying, so I'm here to calm her down and remind her there is nothing to worry about."

"I just really want things to be different now. We are starting our new college life away from home, and I'm afraid I'll end up all alone again. I don't want that."

"Babe, you're not alone. I know you went through a

lot, but you have to trust me that you will have the time of your life. Besides, I'll be with you every step of the way to enjoy it with you," Jace said before kissing the top of Sadie's head.

★★★★★

When Sadie awoke, she found herself all curled up in her bed with her blankets tucked around her and a note on her pillow. It read: "See you in the morning, Sleeping Beauty."

She smiled when she recognized Jace's handwriting, and just like that, she decided that she wasn't going to let her fears and worries get in her way today. She would give it her all to make sure everything went well—no matter what.

Laura, Luke, and Jace were at the table having breakfast when Sadie entered the kitchen.

"Morning, Sadie. Would you like a cup of coffee?" Laura called out as she went to refill her own cup.

"Yes, please," Sadie said as she sat next to Jace.

"Morning, beautiful. Did you sleep well?" he whispered to her.

She smiled as she remembered how she had fallen into a peaceful sleep curled up in Jace's arms. Laura set a cup of coffee in front of her with a blueberry muffin.

"You know, I'm going to miss all of us having breakfast every morning before you guys head off to school while Luke and I go off to work. Breakfast just won't be the same from now on. I'm getting sad just thinking about it already."

Sadie couldn't help but roll her eyes. Her sister was

being so dramatic. "Yeah, right. I bet you guys are going to be plenty busy without a bunch of kids in your way. Am I right, Luke?"

"Look at the time … I'm going to finish loading up the car," Luke said in a hurry as he raced out the kitchen door.

Sadie laughed as she saw him turn bright red right before the door closed behind him. She thought back to how while she was learning to control her gift, she had accidentally read Luke's mind a couple of times. It was always about her sister, and it was definitely stuff she could've gone without knowing. Luke always apologized and was embarrassed, but she wasn't mad at Luke at all. If anything, it was her fault for invading his privacy; however, it was still fun to tease Luke about it at times.

Laura had an annoyed looked directed at her, and Jace had a smirk on his face as he shook his head to stop from laughing out loud.

"Anyway, Jace," Laura continued. "I want you to promise me you will take care of Sadie up there. I'm depending on you."

"Of course, You have nothing to worry about, Laura. She will be in good hands. I've got her back."

"Okay then. I'm going to go finish getting ready. See you in a bit," Laura said, taking her coffee and leaving the room.

"Hey, stop worrying that pretty little head of yours. Trust me, okay? I meant every word I said to Laura. Everything is going to be great," Jace told Sadie as he bumped her shoulder playfully to get her to loosen up a bit.

"I trust you," she answered back.

★★★★★

The drive was only three hours, but it might as well have been six, as time seemed to move so slowly, Sadie thought. They arrived at their new beach apartment around noon, and she couldn't help herself as she went ahead of everyone and unlocked the front door. The apartment was absolutely beautiful with its cream-colored walls, sky-blue couch, and two comfy chairs plus a dark wooden coffee table and a seashell candleholder with three gold candles sitting in the center. One wall had three wooden bookshelves in a line, while the other wall held sliding glass doors directly in front of the ocean.

She could totally see herself having her coffee every morning while watching the waves.

The kitchen had a beautiful light-blue wall, white cabinets, and a white marble countertop with three blue barstools next to it. She was so happy because everything felt so warm and welcoming to her that she couldn't help but put her arms out and spin around n enjoyment.

She felt Jace come up behind her and wrap his arms around her. She closed her eyes and leaned her head against his chest.

"Wow, I'm jealous," Laura said. "Luke, we need to get a summer beach apartment for ourselves." She set a couple of boxes down on the living room floor while her eyes scanned the whole room.

Luke laughed as he set his own boxes on the floor right after her. "Sure, baby, but it won't be for a while. I have other things planned first."

Sadie had to look away or be grossed out as her sister started to wrap her arms around Luke's neck to give him a kiss of appreciation, which she had no desire to see. *They better break that up right after,* Sadie thought to herself, *or unloading the car will take longer than necessary. Plus, I don't want to starve. The sooner we unpack, the sooner we can go to lunch.*

★★★★★

Sadie gave Laura one more final hug goodbye.

"I'm going to miss you," Laura said. "Please call me soon and let me know how your classes are."

She watched Laura's eyes get all watery and emotional, and it really touched her heart.

"I promise I will, but you have to promise me that Luke and you will enjoy yourselves for once and let loose have some fun since you don't have to worry about me and Jace anymore."

Laura laughed and hugged Sadie one more time and then turned to give Jace a hug goodbye. She saw Luke leaning against the car watching with a smile. "Take care of my sister for me, please," She said, walking up to him.

Luke scooped her up in his arms. "You know I will, and if you ever need anything, please don't hesitate to call me. I'll be here for you anytime. You hear me?"

She hugged Luke back as her own way of telling him she loved him. And with one final wave goodbye, Laura and Luke were gone.

"Guess we better go unpack our stuff now and start to get settled," Sadie said as she turned to Jace.

"I've got a better idea. Since it's such a big day and the

ocean is right here, how about we go hit the water for a couple of hours and then unpack later?"

"Okay," she said laughing. She wasn't going to argue besides she had been dying to get into the ocean since they'd arrived.

★★★★★

Five hours later, She loved the beach and just couldn't get enough of it. She finally found her most comfortable pair of gray shorts and a blue tank top after searching her third box and now she was ready to join Jace in the kitchen to unpack.

"I order a pepperoni, mushroom, and bacon pizza and a two-liter of Dr. Pepper," Jace said as he grabbed a box from the living room floor and put it on top of the table.

Sadie couldn't help but think about her classes, since she would be taking a full course load with the end goal of fulfilling her dream of becoming a writer one day. She had secretly been working on her own book for a year now, and not even Jace or Laura knew about it. She still wasn't sure if it was any good and was way too scared to find out the truth, so she figured the more work she put in during college, the faster she would reach her goal and finally feel more confident about and herself and her book.

"Do you have football practice tomorrow morning?" she asked Jace.

"Yeah, are you still coming with me?"

"Yep, I'm going to check out the campus and see where everything is so I'm better prepared."

The semester didn't really start until Monday, but

Jace's coach wanted to meet with his new team on Friday so they could get the meet and greet out of the way and get right to work when the semester started.

"We can grab lunch afterward," Jace said with a smile.

She nodded as she grabbed all her favorite picture frames and went to the bookshelves in the living room. It wouldn't feel like home until the photos of all the people she truly loved and cared about were around her. The first photo was of her parents having one of their usual moonlight walk down the beach during their summer vacations. After their parents' deaths, Sadie begged Laura for the picture and had kept it with her ever since because looking at the picture always made her happy.

The second photo was of Laura and Luke laughing and cuddling on the couch. They had all been hanging out one day when Sadie snapped the picture. She felt like the picture showed how happy her sister and Luke were and how in love they were. Laura still had that look of being completely in love even so many years down the road. Luke obviously felt the same way about Laura.

There were a ton of pictures of Jace and Sadie, but she had three that she absolutely loved the most. The first picture of Jace and her at the county fair riding the Ferris wheel and smiling like they were on top of the world since it was their favorite ride so every year they rode it at least once—sometimes more like five times. Second was of Jace smiling pushing her on a swing at the park when they were still little kids, she was laughing with her arms extended like she was flying. She really did like the feeling of being up high in the air, It made her feel so free and powerful all at the same time.

The third and by far her favorite had been taken at the end of their last high school football game after Jace had made the winning touchdown. That night changed everything for her future. It all started when she noticed that Jace was talking to the school principal and a bunch of other gentlemen periodically during the game. When Jace smiled and shook hands with the gentlemen and principal, he ran to the bleachers, grabbed her, and wrapped her up in his embrace, whispering that they would be going to college together since he'd received a full scholarship for football. The photo that Laura took that night showed Sadie with a huge smile on her face and Jace's arms wrapped around her from behind as he kissed her cheek. The whole picture captured the perfect moment of happiness to her.

"Hey, pizza's here," Jace called out. His voice brought her back to reality and her hungry stomach.

★★★★★

It was about midnight when she was standing in Jace's bedroom doorway. She couldn't sleep in her new room and she didn't know what it was exactly, maybe being in a new apartment or living in a new city. Whatever it was, it put her on edge and she didn't want to sleep alone, so she put on her best sad puppy-dog look and hoped for mercy.

"I was wondering when you were going to show up," Jace said with a smirk as he was lying in his bed with his hands behind his head.

He knew her so well so without another word, she turned off the light, crawled into bed, and made herself cozy. Jace wrapped his arms around her stomach and pulled her toward him.

"Now let's get some sleep. We have a big day tomorrow," Jace said before giving her a quick kiss on the neck

CHAPTER 2

J ACE HAD LEFT TO MEET with his coach and teammates, and in the twenty minutes since he'd left, Sadie realized just how big the campus was. She was going to be getting a ton of exercise from all the walking she would be doing. So far, she had managed to find all her classes, plus the college bookstore and the Seaside Café.

She had to admit it did seem kind of nerdy to find all her classes ahead of time now that she was college, but she was willing to do just about anything to make sure things were different from her past. This was her chance to make the life she wanted, and she had no plans of messing things up.

"Hey, beautiful, you must be new. I haven't seen you before."

Wow … Did I hear that right? Sadie thought as she turned and saw a really cute dark-haired guy leaning against the café wall looking at her.

"Um … hi." This guy was completely hot, and as she looked around and behind her, as she realized there was no one else around. This hot guy was actually talking to her of all people. She couldn't believe it. No one besides Jace and her sister had ever called her beautiful, and in all honesty, it felt really good.

"What's your name?" the guy asked.

Oh my God. Sadie couldn't think. Her nerves were getting to her, and she suddenly felt very warm—borderline hot.

"I have to go," she said before running off.

"See you around then," the cute guy called out after her.

That was enough sightseeing for one day, she thought as she made her way to the football field feeling confused and a little disappointed in herself.

★★★★★

"Hey, babe, you ready for lunch?" Jace asked.

She looked at her watch and was shocked. She must have lost track of time because it felt like she had just been sitting on the bleachers waiting for Jace to finish, but now she realize an hour had passed.

"Yeah, sure. Where do you want to go?" she asked as she put her book back in her bag.

"Some of the guys said the café on campus is pretty good. Want to check it out?"

The cute guy from earlier came to mind, and her nervousness came back as well. She couldn't help but wonder if he was still there, and it made her feel like her stomach was turning inside and out.

"Um … No. Can we go somewhere near the beach instead?"

"Sure. Is everything all right?" Jace asked with a look of concern.

"Yeah, of course. Let's go before we starve," she answered with a laugh.

They found a cute Mexican restaurant right on the bay and found an open table on the patio.

"So what are your new coach and teammates like?" Sadie asked as she began to scan the menu.

"They're all pretty cool guys and easy to get along with. What about you? Did you find all your classes?"

The waiter had dropped off their drinks and then took their orders before leaving the table. She still couldn't get the cute guy from the café out of her mind. He was incredibly good looking and had wanted to talk to her, and she ran away like a coward. She felt like a huge disappointment.

Suddenly, Sadie snapped back to Jace and his question. "Yeah. The campus is huge, but I managed to find all my classes plus the bookstore, so I'm totally ready for the semester to start. What about you? Do you know where all your classes are going to be?"

"Nah, I'll just wing it like I usually do … Sadie, is there something wrong?"

She should've of known that she couldn't hide anything from her best friend. Jace knew her too well. Sometimes it was weird how in tune he was with her feelings, but it was also very comforting.

"It's probably nothing, but there was this guy who said hi to me today, and I got scared and ran away like a chicken. I'm just disappointed in myself, and I didn't want to bother you with it because I always seem afraid of everything. But there's no need to worry. Hey ... how about we do something together tonight?"

"Sure," Jace agreed. "What do you have in mind?"

"I don't know. How about a movie and then a walk on the beach afterward. You interested?"

Jace smirked at her. "Sure, I'm game"

"Great. I just happen to know exactly what movie we should see." She smiled as she bit into her taco. She'd been wanting to see the movie she had in mind for a long time.

★★★★★

"Sadie, are you almost ready?" Jace called from the living room.

"Yeah," she yelled back as she took one more look at herself in the mirror. She had decided on her dark-purple sundress and brown leather ankle boots, and let her hair flow down her back in waves. She was totally satisfied with her look as she headed to the living room with confidence.

When they got to the theater, Jace got in line to buy snacks, while She grabbed the seats on the very top. It was their favorite spot to sit when they went to the movies.

"Well hello again. Imagine us running into each other twice in one day."

Sadie froze and then slowly turned only to see the same guy from earlier looking at her from the aisle. He looked even hotter than before, now dressed in in a gray button-down shirt, faded blue jeans, and black boots. Now that he was closer, She saw his hair was dark brown and cut short and tight. His hazel eyes were nice too.

Okay, she said to herself. *It's time to stop being a chicken and woman up.* "Hi," she said aloud.

"Hello. We didn't get a chance to introduce ourselves last time. I'm Adam. What's your name?"

"I'm Sadie,"

"Nice to meet you, Sadie. Are you here to see this movie all by yourself? If so, I'll keep you company if you like."

"No, she isn't."

As Adam turned, Sadie saw Jace standing behind him with their snacks. She wanted to get up and help Jace, but she felt strong tension and animosity, so instead, she sat and watched. Jace continue to stare at Adam and say nothing. He simply smiled and started back down the aisle like nothing happen.

Adam stopped two steps down and turned back around. "See you later, Sadie."

Just like that, it was over. Adam didn't wait for a response. He just headed down the aisle.

Jace came up and took his seat. He handed Sadie the bag of popcorn and put the soda in the cup holder between them.

"Do you know that guy?" he asked.

"He was the guy I told you about earlier at the campus café. I just know now that his name is Adam."

Jace's eyes went back to Adam who had sat four rows down. She wanted to ask him what was going on, but something told her not to.

"Forget about it. Let's enjoy the movie," he said, slinging his arm around the back of her chair without another word.

★★★★★

Sadie took her boots off as soon as she could to feel the sand between her toes.

"Did you enjoy the movie?" Jace asked as he handed her an ice-cream cone.

"Yes. I loved it,"

She licked her rocky road cone as Jace got his usual pistachio cone.

"You know, the girl in the movie reminded me a lot of you."

She took that as a compliment because the girl in the movie was a classical musician who was not afraid to go after her dreams. It was obvious that the girl in the movie played with a pure passion for the music and nothing more. She really wanted to be just like her—if only she could tackle her fears. The one thing that Sadie had learned painfully since her parents' passing was that fear is its own monster, and the longer you ignore it, the bigger the monster becomes. Pretty soon, the fear becomes so big you don't know how to overcome it.

There was a bright light halfway down the beach, and if she had to guess, Sadie would say it was a bonfire.

"Hey, Jace," a guy called out to them.

"Hey, Evan. What's up, man?"

"Nothing much. Just having a little bonfire before the season starts. You guys want to join us?"

Sadie looked at Evan and thought he looked like a typical football player—very tall and muscular. He had black hair and blue eyes.

"Do you want to?" Jace asked her.

She could tell by the look on his face that he wanted to go, so how could she say no? "Okay,"

"Yeah, man," Jace told Evan. "We will join you guys. This is my best girl Sadie."

"Hey, Sadie. I'm Evan, and this is Nick, Brandon, and his girlfriend, Ashley, over there."

Sadie looked over at the only other girl at the bonfire. She was a tall, pretty redhead with light-brown eyes and a pale skin tone. What was striking was the color of Ashley's hair because it reminded her of a bright-red apple. It was pretty cool to look at.

"Hi," Sadie said to everyone.

She followed Jace to an open spot by Brandon and Ashley. She had to admit, it was extremely nerve-racking sitting with a bunch of people she didn't know. All She could do was hoped that her gift didn't cause her to have a panic attack in front of them—*that* would suck.

"Hey, you guys want a beer?" Nick called out to them.

"No, man. We're good, but if you've got a couple of waters, we would take those."

Nick nodded and reached in the cooler.

"Hi. I'm Ashley Fin, So where are you and Jace from? All Brandon told me was that Jace is the new guy and that he's pretty cool. You know how men are with so few words."

"Hi, nice to meet you, we're from Yuma, Arizona."

Ashley made a sour face and stuck her tongue out. "Isn't it super hot there?"

Sadie couldn't help but laugh. She guessed that Ashley had absolutely no idea just how hot it could get in Yuma. "Actually, it can reach over a hundred degrees during the summers ... and sometimes it's even hotter than that,"

"That is way too hot for me. I've lived in San Diego all my life and don't ever plan on leaving. You know, we should do coffee sometime, and I can introduce you to some friends of mine."

"Sure. That would be great," Sadie said without a second thought. She could already see that Ashley was fun to talk to, and besides she knew she needed to face her fears about meeting new people. Plus, it was really cute to watch Brandon whisper things into Ashley's ear that would make her giggle and then lean in for a kiss.

★★★★★

She was genuinely happy. Jace was living up to his word, things were way different, and she was enjoying everything.

"Nice entrance," Jace said with a laugh as she curled up under the covers when he got back in bed from turning off the light. She felt him relax behind her as he wrapped his arm around her stomach.

"Did you have fun today, baby?" he asked.

She smiled and nodded because she'd actually had a great day. However, the mysterious Adam was on her mind, and she couldn't help but hope she'd see him again.

CHAPTER 3

SADIE COULD TELL THAT IT was still early by the sunlight that was creeping up on the window when she opened her eyes. It was the perfect time for her first morning run on the beach, so she quietly slid out of bed and tiptoed to her room so she could change into workout clothes.

★★★★★

As Sadie neared the apartment complex after her run, she couldn't believe her eyes. *What is he doing here? And, more importantly, how does he know where I live?*

Adam was smiling as she walked up to him. "Good morning," he said.

"Hi ... How do you know where I live?"

"Well, you see, I was kind of already hanging out at the beach when I saw you start your run out of this apartment, so I thought I would just wait until you got back. I figured maybe we could talk."

He was at the beach around six o'clock in the morning wearing jeans, a white shirt, and black boots? He wasn't dressed to work out, and he didn't look like a typical beach guy or a surfer; however, he did look good, and Sadie really wanted to talk to him for some reason. In that moment, she decided it was time to swallow her fear.

"Okay," she said. "I'm game. Let's talk."

"Well, I know you just came back from a run, but would you be willing to take a walk with me at the water's edge? I think you will be surprised to learn that I'm not such a bad guy."

"Okay. Let's go then,"

It felt strange. The quietness she had enjoyed only moments ago now seemed unsettling with Adam behind her. She always loved it when it was just her and the ocean, but now it caused her to feel jittery. She told herself to be brave and confident and not let the fear win. It sounded easy, but in truth, it was a lot harder than it sounded.

When Sadie reached the water's edge, she swallowed down her fear and turned toward Adam. He was looking directly at her with an adorable smirk on his face.

"You know, you are quite beautiful," he said.

Talk about being thrown off her game. Sadie couldn't help but blush at his remark. He had to be kidding. Sadie thought she was anything but beautiful in that moment, no makeup and drenched in sweat.

"Thank you, but I'm sure you didn't wait for me all this time just to tell me I'm beautiful. So what did you want to talk about?" Sadie questioned.

"A girl who gets right to the point, I like that. If you must know, there is something about you that is different from most girls, and I can't get you out of my mind."

"Wow. Do you use those lines on all the girls?"

"Just the girls who I find interesting, and right now, you are the only interesting girl I see," Adam told her.

"How do you know I'm interesting? You just met me."

Adam smiled and closed the distance between them by a few feet. "I can tell that you are interesting and sexy just by looking at you."

"I'm not used to hearing that. You make me nervous when you say such over-the-top things."

"Well, you shouldn't be nervous. Come on, Sadie … What do you say? Are you going to give me a chance? Trust me. I don't bite."

★★★★★

"Rise and shine, sleepyhead. It's time to get up for the day."

Sadie stirred at the sound of Jace's voice in her ear, and the aroma of freshly brewed coffee was all around her.

"Good morning," she said. "Is that for me?"

"Of course. I know my girl loves her coffee first thing in the morning."

"Thanks." She closed her eyes in enjoyment of the first rich sip of hazelnut and caffeine that traveled down her throat.

"So how about we finish our unpacking and then hit the store for food and any other supplies that we need?" Jace suggested.

"Cool with me. Let's get started," she said as she stretched her whole body out before hopping out of bed.

"I woke up without you next to me,"

She had showered and gotten into her bed to close her eyes and rest for a bit and probably dozed off shortly after. As she recalled her morning, Adam came to mind, and she had to admit she'd really enjoyed herself. They'd talked about everything, and Adam had made her laugh so much it was unbelievable. She struggled with whether to tell Jace about their encounter. He hadn't been happy when he'd seen Adam at the theater, but that could've been her fault for the first impression she'd given off when telling Jace about Adam. She really needed to stop and think before she said stuff. That had always been a problem of hers. She had a tendency of just saying what she felt or saw and would only later realize that she'd put her foot in her mouth. Then have to apologize.

Sadie looked up. "I woke up early and went for a run. You know me … I couldn't pass up the opportunity now that we live so close to the ocean."

"Yeah, I kind of figured that was where you went," Jace said with a laugh as he got up and announced that he was going to get breakfast started for them.

Sadie felt major guilt lying to her best friend. She had never lied to Jace before, but she had to admit that she'd really enjoyed spending time with Adam more than she thought possible. They had a lot in common—movies they'd seen and books they'd read—and he was so funny. Sadie was already looking forward to seeing him again, but now was not the time to be thinking about that. She had to get ready for her day with Jace and devote her attention to her best friend. Maybe she could fix her mistake, and Jace could give Adam a chance and realize he wasn't such a bad guy after all.

★★★★★

By the time Sadie and Jace finally made it to the grocery store, it was after eight o'clock in the evening. They decided to split up and get everything they needed so they could hurry back home to relax and watch a movie during a late dinner.

She headed in the direction of the fruit but wasn't paying attention to where she was going and ran right into the chest of a large man. She was about to apologize for being so inconsiderate when she was suddenly hit with overwhelming thoughts of anger and hatred. The man's mind was overflowing her mind with all his thoughts, and it hurt as she realized he was a monster.

This man constantly belittled and called his girlfriend names and even slapped and pushed her around, saying she deserved it. According to him, women had one role, and that was to serve the men in their lives. If they failed, they deserved some kind of punishment to make them learn from their mistakes because to him women were nothing more than slaves. The most recent incident had been earlier that day when he had woken her up, grabbed his girlfriend's arms, and slapped her across the face. He'd been thinking the bitch had gotten off easy and being so lazy

Sadie could feel the woman shaking with fear and was too afraid to do anything. It almost felt like he had slapped her himself.

Suddenly, Sadie found herself bent over and holding her stomach as tears rolled down her cheeks.

"What the hell is wrong with you?" the man asked.

It sounded like the guy was yelling, but she realized that may be because of the sense of anger she felt from his tone. She hadn't moved since the fear had consumed her, but Sadie quickly realized that if he was that awful to his girlfriend, she didn't want to find out how he'd treat someone he didn't know at all. She quickly stepped away, dropping the fruit she bagged in the nearest bin, and ran to the restroom where she locked herself in a stall and began to cry as she was trembling uncontrollably. This was exactly why she didn't want this in her life. Why suffer through somebody else's pain? All she wanted was to be left alone.

★★★★★

She never told Jace what happened at the store. Instead, she pushed it to the back of her mind so she could focus on her first day of college. As first days went, she enjoyed herself and liked every class she had. And yet, she still kept thinking about the guy at the store and the way he was treating his girlfriend—and probably any other girl in his life. No matter how much Sadie told herself it wasn't her responsibility, guilt weighed heavy on her shoulders for doing nothing when she could've done something.

She needed to focus, since she was facing her worst enemy ever. No matter how hard she studied, it just never made sense to her. She swore that math hated her.

"Sadie."

She turned around smiling, excited to hear that voice. "Hi, Adam."

"Is this seat taken? Or is your boyfriend going to pop up behind me again?" he said while pretending to look around each corner expecting Jace to step out of nowhere.

"No, it's not taken, and Jace isn't my boyfriend. He's my best friend since childhood," she said laughing.

"That is the best news I have heard today," he said as he took the seat next to her.

"So how was the rest of your weekend? The highlight of mine was taking a nice walk on the beach with a beautiful girl. How about you, Did you have any fun this weekend?"

She couldn't help buy blush because their walk was one of the best parts of her weekend as well. She became so happy over the weekend just thinking about it and the fun they'd had. She couldn't help but look forward to spending more time with him.

She was so lost in thought that she gasped when she felt his fingers under her chin tilting her head up. A sudden burst of pain exploded in her head as the thoughts of everyone in the room flooded her mind at once. She was so wrapped up in Adam's words, and his touch was consuming her body in such a way that the protection around her mind began to crack. This is what she always feared about her gift and what she and Laura had worked so hard to avoid.

As she looked around the classroom, all kinds of things were coming into her mind at once: someone having a bad breakup, happiness over a current GPA, drama over a fight with a friend ... But what confused her most of all was this strong desire, almost like a pure physical desire of ownership. She started to feel lightheaded from the pain and knew she had to get herself under control quickly or it would get worse. She jerked her chin away and closed her eyes tightly and started to take several deep breaths to calm herself while trying not to think about how Adam was looking at her right now.

When the professor decided to start the lecture, Sadie thanked the heavens as she was then able to focus on rebuilding the wall around her mind. She and Laura had come up with an exercise for her mind that created a barrier to keep everyone else's thoughts out. It wasn't perfect because there was always a constant annoying buzz in her head, but that was better than being continuously bombarded by other people's thoughts and emotions. Sadie was relieved she didn't have to look at Adam at that moment, because she thought she must look like a freak. Still, she could feel his stare.

★★★★★

Jace had football practice, so she had planned to head home after class and call Laura. She also wanted to do something special for dinner, so she grabbed her books and bag and began to run out the door. She really didn't want to see that look, since she was still embarrassed from before. She already knew it was always the same look from everyone was trying to figure out if she was crazy. She especially didn't want to see it from a guy she was actually starting to like.

"Sadie," Adam called after her

She bit her bottom lip as she turned to face him, but when she looked into Adam's eyes, she was surprised to see something entirely different. It froze her where she stood.

"I don't know what happened earlier, and I can see you don't want to talk about it, which is fine, but I want you to know it doesn't discourage my interest in you whatsoever." Adam smiled as he squeezed her hand before letting go and walking out the door.

Sadie was speechless. That had never happened before. Usually everyone thought she was crazy afterward. She needed to talk to her sister ASAP.

The first thing she did when she got home was change into a tank top and shorts, and then made herself comfortable on the couch so she could call her sister.

"Hey, Laura," she said after her sister picked up on the second ring.

"Hey," Laura answered. "How was your first day?"

"It was pretty good. I like most of my classes—except math"

"Yeah, that sounds like you. How's Jace?"

"He likes his new team. He's at practice right now."

"I'm glad that you guys are enjoying yourselves up there."

"Yeah, me too, but I need to talk to you about something important."

"Sure. What's up?" Laura asked.

"Okay … this might seem kind of random because I've never asked you before. But where does our family gift come from, and why do we have it?"

"Wow. I really never imagined you asking me that," Laura admitted. "Well, I really don't know all the details except what Mom told me once. She was always saying that it's important that we help people and that we should try our best. Our family has carried this gift for generations."

There was a pause on the other end of the phone

before Laure continued. "There was this one time when Mom and I went to the downtown market, and I thought it was a little weird that she kept looking at this one specific elderly woman. The woman kept walking around, but it looked like she was just going through the motions and not really caring about anything. She kept looking at things but not buying anything. The next thing I knew, Mom walked over and started talking to her. I thought it was Mom just being nice, but when we went to visit the same elderly woman another time, the woman told me something that made me realize what she had done.

"She had said, 'You know, sweetheart, you are blessed with a wonderful mother. She saved my life and the loneliness that was around me since my husband passed away. John and I were together for forty years. He was my soul mate, and I was devastated when he passed. All I wanted was to see my John again until your mother came to me and taught me how to live again. Your mother is my guardian angel.'"

Sadie felt ashamed listening to how selfless their mom had been. While all she had been doing was thinking about herself and the guy from the grocery store came to mind, and Sadie flinched even more as she wondered how disappointed her mother would be knowing she had done nothing at all.

"Why didn't you tell me this before?" Sadie questioned.

"I know I should have, but you were so young when Mom and Dad passed away. I thought it would be better to teach you how to block the gift and give you a chance at some sort of normal life instead of having you deal with all that responsibility. Then you had found Jace, and you were so happy. I just didn't want to ruin that.

"In truth that wasn't the only reason that I did what I did ... Mom told me something horrible that scared me. You were all the family I had left, and I didn't want to lose you too."

"What did she say?"

"That doing something for one person can also cause a negative effect for another if you are not careful. There is always an equal reaction to everything a person does."

Sadie couldn't help but feel a cold shiver travel down her back. *What is that supposed to mean?* she wondered. "Mom didn't say anything else?" Sadie asked.

"I never got the chance to ask. The accident happened a week later, and shortly after, I noticed the gift had started to pass to you. You were so sad and afraid, and all I thought of was Mom's warning. I'm sorry, Sadie."

"Laura, it's okay. I understand why you did it, and I know Mom and Dad would be proud of how strong you have become."

"Thanks. That means more than you know."

When Sadie looked at the clock, she was surprised to see it was almost six o'clock. They had been on the phone for almost two hours, and she needed to get dinner started. She told Laura goodbye and promised to call her again soon.

Although Sadie felt a little better after talking with her sister, it also gave her plenty to think about.

★★★★★

"Something smells good," Jace called out as he walked in the apartment an hour later.

Sadie had just finished setting the plates of Mongolian beef and steamed brown rice on the table. "I hope you're hungry," she said.

"Are you kidding? I'm starving," he said leaning in and kissing her cheek before going to wash his hands.

"Did you have a good practice?" she asked as she sat down.

"Yeah, we have a game in a couple of weeks. How was your day?" he asked sitting down opposite of her.

"I like all my classes except math, of course."

"You've got nothing to worry about. I've got your back on that."

"Thanks, but what about your classes?" she asked.

"They're good," Jace answered. "Nothing I can't handle"

Jace was always like that—never afraid of a challenge. He faced anything head on with no fear. She wished she could be like that one day, but until that time came, at least she had him by her side.

★★★★★

When Sadie opened her eyes, she saw Jace leaning over her.

"It's late," he said. "Do you want to go to sleep with me or stay here?"

She looked around at her notebooks all open on her bed with her books. After dinner, she'd gone to her room to study and figured she must have fallen asleep. She wrap her arms around Jace's neck as he scooped her up in his arms and carried her to his room. As soon as she hit the bed, she instantly fell back to sleep.

★★★★★

The waves were crashing in front of her, and the sea breeze was all around and then she heard a familiar voice. "Hi, honey."

Sadie froze with fear. She hadn't heard that voice for almost ten years. Slowly, she turned around and forced herself to blink a couple of times to make sure what she was seeing was real. "Mom?"

"Yes, honey. I'm here." That was all she needed to hear, and she instantly ran into her mother's arms and cried like a baby.

"Calm down, sweetie," her mom said while rubbing her back.

"Why are you here, Mom? How is this possible?"

"I'm here to help, of course. Come on … Let's sit down, and we can talk."

"Mom, you must be really disappointed in me," Sadie said with a sigh. "I'm so sorry."

"No, honey. You have nothing to apologize for. You were so young, and I wasn't there for you when you needed me the most. I am the one who's sorry," her mom said, trying her best to reassure her.

"Mom, how did you do it? How could you let everything in and not become overwhelmed?"

"At first, I was just as overwhelmed as you are. In fact, all I wanted was for it to all go away, but my mother didn't want to hear that. She tried to teach me the importance and responsibilities of carrying the gift. Sadly, I didn't want to hear it. I thought if I ignored it enough, maybe it would go away on its own. But, much to my dismay, it didn't, and then a tragic incident forced me to open my eyes and realize my mistake.

"Her name was Hannah and she was a classmate of mine during high school. She was a quiet girl who didn't talk much, and a lot of kids made fun of her since she was poor. I didn't think much of it at first, because we weren't really friends. I hardly knew her; plus, at the time all I wanted was a moment of peace and quiet from all the thoughts invading my mind. I should've paid attention better. I'll always regret that I didn't.

I read her mind by accident, and one thought came to me loud and clear: *I wish I'd never existed. Nobody would miss me.* "There was so much pain with her, and I didn't need or want any of it so, I ran home and tried to block out everything. The next day during homeroom, Hannah's chair was empty, and for some reason, I had an awful feeling. That day I found Hannah's address and went to her house and when I arrived, I found her little sister sitting on a tire swing all by herself with tears streaming from her eyes. When I approached her and asked if Hannah was home, the little girl began to sob and told me Hannah had hung herself in her bedroom last night. She was gone forever. I felt like I was going to throw up right there. I knew I'd heard her plea the day before and did absolutely nothing to help.

"That was when I started to wonder what kind of person I was because she was right there next to me and I let her die for no reason. When I told my mom what happened, she was very disappointed in me since she had repeatedly explain the responsibilities to me and I just wouldn't listened. Hannah's life was gone, and I had made the biggest mistake of my life. After that day I worked extra hard to help as many people as I could to make sure that what happened to Hannah wouldn't happen to anybody else."

The tears that filled Sadie's eyes began to roll down her cheeks. "Mom, I miss you and Dad so much. I wish you guys were still here."

"I know, honey. All I can say is that everything happens for a reason. Life is what you make of it. I had the best life because it brought me you and your sister. I wouldn't trade that for anything. Your father and I are very proud of you both, and you have our blessings in whatever you two decide to do with your lives."

"I love you guys so much," Sadie said as her mother slowly faded away.

★★★★★

Sadie opened her eyes and reached over to shake Jace awake.

"What's wrong?" he asked as he looked over at her with concern.

Sadie couldn't hold it in anymore and started to cry as Jace wrapped his arms around her and held her close. She finally told him everything about class, her call with Laura, and now her dream with her mom. It was a lot to take in.

"I'd never realized how important my family gift was," she said. "My mom was so strong to stand up after such a tragedy. I hope I can be just as strong."

"Wait, what are you saying?" Jace questioned.

"I don't know," "I just think I owe it to my mom to at least try to help people like she did."

"I don't want anything bad to happen to you."

"I don't want that either, but I can't help to think about what my mom went through. As her daughter, I should be just as strong as she was—or try to be."

"Okay, but I want to know everything, No secrets."

"Of course, You're my best friend after all."

"Let's go back to sleep then."

As she cuddled back into Jace's arms, she had to admit she was scared. What if she wasn't as strong as her mom? She felt Jace's arm wrap around her stomach, and she smiled closing her eyes and deciding to, forget her worries for a little awhile at least.

CHAPTER 4

SADIE FIGURED THE LIBRARY WAS a good place to start. She noticed all the people at the bookshelves looking at books, while others were texting on their cell phones. One person in particular caught her attention. It looked like she had about twenty different art books open all over the table, and she was typing all kinds of information into her laptop. It had to be one hell of a test or paper that she was working on because she looked beyond stressed and exhausted.

It's now or never, Sadie thought as she took a huge breath and headed over to the table. She quietly pulled out the chair in front of the girl and set her book bag down on the table. "You look like you're studying hard there. Art history major?"

The girl looked up from her laptop and smiled. "Yeah, I love art. It's kind of a passion of mine."

"I took an art history class once and really enjoy it. Is that the career field you are trying to pursue?" Sadie asked as she focused on the girl's mind.

"Yeah."

If everything goes according to plan. I should be in New York by next year if I can secure that internship.

Sadie wanted to smile in triumphant as the girl thoughts floated in her mind, but that probably wouldn't be appropriated. Instead, she masked her emotion and thought about what her mom would do next in this situation. "Would you like some help studying?" Sadie asked.

"Thanks. That's very nice of you, but I'm sure you probably have your own work that you need to be doing."

"No, not really. I was just working on a psychology paper, but it's not do for a while," Said told her. "Besides, this looks really important to you, and I would love to help. Who knows, maybe you can teach me something about art history that I never learn before."

"Wow, that's really nice of you. I guess it would help with the exam coming up," the girl admitted. "My name is Jenny Phillips, by the way."

"It's nice to meet you. I'm Sadie James, Shall we get started?"

Jenny smiled and nodded while handing over one of the books to Sadie. "Could you quiz me on these paintings?"

In that moment, Sadie finally understood why her mom decided to help people because even with this small act, she felt great. It might not change the world, but it would change someone's life for the better, and that was okay with her.

★★★★★

"Hey, beautiful. What are you doing?"

Sadie looked up and was surprised to see Adam. This guy always showed up when she least expected it.

"Hey, Adam, Jenny and I are studying art history. What's up with you?"

"Looking for you, of course. I never saw you during our break, and you never made it to class."

Shit, Sadie thought to herself. She'd forgotten about class. She was so engrossed helping Jenny study that she must have lost track of time. And it was math class too. She couldn't afford to miss any class, since she had a hard enough time with her work as it is. Maybe she could talk to the professor and see if he could help her out with some study guides.

"No worries," Adam said, interrupting her thoughts. "I have the assignment and all the notes for today. Do you want to go grab a bite to eat, and we can talk?"

"Go ahead, Sadie," Jenny said. "You've already help me so much. I'm more than ready now, and I can't thank you enough for that."

"Okay, but only if you are sure," Sadie responded. "You have my number now, and I want to know the second you get that internship so we can do something to celebrate."

Jenny smiled and nodded. "I feel New York is in the bag now. Thank you."

★★★★★

Adam took Sadie to the campus café and grabbed a shaded table outside. "Have you had a chance to eat here yet?" he asked.

"No, not really," she said, feeling a little guilty

about being there with Adam after rejecting Jace's lunch suggestion.

"Well that's perfect considering this is where I first saw you."

She learned that the café sold a variety of sandwiches, soups, salads, and pastries. She decided to get herself a cup of vegetable soup with a small chicken Caesar salad and an ice water, while Adam got a turkey sandwich with chips and a pop.

"I'm glad you decided to have a bite to eat with me," Adam noted.

"Yeah, why's that?" Sadie asked.

"It gives me a chance to know you better, and since we never got to the awkward questions last time, I say let's do that now. So how do you like living in San Diego?"

She couldn't help but smile before responding. "Yeah, I really do like it here. I've always dreamed about living here."

"So, ocean girl, how long have you known Jace?"

Why is he interested in my relationship with Jace? she thought to herself before answering. "We grew up together."

One thing was sure: it was different sitting here with Adam. Of course, the feeling of keeping her gift a secret was there, but there was also a wave of confidence flowing through her from being near him. He somehow made her feel like her own person in a way.

"So does your family live in San Diego?" she asked, figuring it was only fair that he should get some awkward questions too. Besides, she really wanted to know the answer.

"No. We're not that close. It's just me … Why? You want to keep me company?" he asked with a smirk.

Sadie couldn't help but smile at that remark. She actually found it a little shocking that she was smiling so much, but it felt so natural and good to be in Adam's presence.

"That was a sexy smile," Adam added. "Sure wouldn't mind seeing that again."

"What are you going to school for?"

"Right now I'm just doing my generals, and then I'll see what interests me after. What about you?"

"English literature," she said with pride.

"Let me guess … You want to be a writer one day."

She couldn't help but blush. It was a little unsettling that he read her so easily.

"You know, we could spend the whole day together," he suggested.

As tempting as that sounded, it wasn't the right thing to do. "Unfortunately, I will have to take a rain check. I have some homework that I need to catch up on. So can I please get those notes and the assignment from class?"

"Of course. I'm a man of my word."

Sadie was a little relieved and disappointed that her time with Adam was over, but she really did need to head home and start studying as soon as possible.

As she stood up to leave, Adam gently took her arm and turned her around. "I really enjoyed myself today, and I'm looking forward to much more." He then leaned over and lightly kissed her cheek.

Sadie blushed as a warm sensation came over her. "I had fun as well," she said.

Sadie turned to leave but stopped dead in her tracks when she saw who was leaning against the wall.

"Jace," she gasped.

"Hey, babe," Jace said, wrapping her up in his arms for a hug.

She hugged him back tightly. It felt good to have his arms around her. "I wasn't expecting to see you until later tonight."

"No practice today, so I thought I'd go find my girl."

"See you later, Sadie," Adam said as he walked past her.

She could feel Jace freeze at that moment, and he locked eyes on Adam as he walk away.

"Isn't that the guy from the theater?" Jace asked. "You didn't tell me he was in one of your classes."

"Yeah, well I was surprised too," Sadie said.

"Is he bothering you?" Jace asked, slightly angry.

"Well, not really. At first it was uncomfortable, but now that we've talked, it's not so bad."

She could see Jace tense up. "Are you sure?"

"Yeah, Is there something wrong?"

"I don't like that guy, and I would prefer if you didn't talk to him."

That's weird. This is not like Jace at all, Sadie thought. He had such a look of anger directed at a guy he didn't even know. She had never seen him do that before. Honestly he had always tried to get her to come out of her shell and make friends and now, he doesn't like the first person she actually opens up to. For a moment, Jace just stared at her, and it almost felt like he was making sure she understood what he was saying so all she could do was remain quiet.

"How do you feel about going to a party with me tonight?" he asked

"Sure," she said, confused by the sudden topic change. Sadie didn't want to question it, though. She wanted Jace to be happy, so she was willing to go to a party just to see him smile and not be so tense.

"It's a guy on the team's girlfriend. She is throwing herself a birthday party on the beach and invited the whole team."

Jace slung his arm around Sadie as they walked. She felt better when she felt his warmth engulf her.

★★★★★

As she went to grab a bottle of water from the fridge, Jace's arm wrapped around her waist and turned her to face him.

"Hey, I'm sorry if I sounded like an ass earlier. Don't be mad. I'm just worried about your safety. You're my girl, and I want to protect you is all."

She knew he meant what he said. It wasn't that she was mad at him, if anything, she was more confused than anything, but she kept that to herself. She had a better idea to take his mind off this uncomfortable subject.

"I understand and I have great news to share with you."

"Oh yeah? What's up?" Jace asked as he ran his fingers through her hair.

"I used my gift and actually helped someone today. It was small, but it was still something," she said with a victorious smile.

"What? Are you okay? Tell me what happened." Jace

asked one question after another as he led her to the couch.

She laughed and curled up to his side before telling him everything from start to finish, including how awesome it felt afterward.

"Wow, babe. I'm proud of you."

Now that sounded liked the Jace she'd known all her life. The guy who always gave her confidence and believed she could do anything. Sadie smiled as she made herself comfortable. The last thing she remembered was Jace's fingers running through her hair before she drifted off to sleep.

★★★★★

"How long was I asleep?" Sadie asked, rubbing her eyes awake.

"Just a couple of hours," Jace told her.

"I'm sorry," she said as she started to sit up and check her hair.

"Don't be. It was nice watching you sleep."

"But what about the party?"

"We have plenty of time. The party doesn't start until ten, and it's only seven. Besides, I was thinking if you want to go get ready, we could go grab something to eat beforehand."

"Okay."

★★★★★

Sadie finally decided on a green sundress with an embroidered brown belt that ended midthigh and her strappy sandals embroidered with white seashells. She pulled her hair up in a high, loose ponytail with her yellow Hawaiian flower clip on the side and added light eye shadow and lip gloss.

"Wow, you look beautiful," Jace said as he stared at her from head to toe when she entered the living room.

"Thanks," she said. She noticed Jace was wearing a pair of tan cargo shorts, a black shirt, and black flip-flops. He actually looked really cute. "So, where are we going to eat? Because I'm starved."

★★★★★

After dinner, Jace and Sadie made their way to the party. Sadie looked around and estimated there were at least fifty to sixty people there. It felt like her stomach dropped to her feet, and that wasn't a good thing considering she'd just eaten a full dinner. She couldn't help but squeeze Jace's hand for a little reassurance that he was with her. She felt him automatically squeeze her hand back, telling her to relax.

"Hey, Jace."

"Hey, Dylan," Jace called back as he made the way to another bonfire where there was a guy with a cute blonde wrap around him. "Hi, Bobby."

"Hey, man. Glad you could make it," Bobby said with a smile.

"Yeah. This is Sadie," Jace said, introducing Sadie to his new friends.

"Hey, Sadie, I'm Bobby, and this is my birthday girl, Chloe."

"Hi, Chloe," Sadie said. "Happy birthday."

"Thanks," Chloe responded.

"There is beer, soda, and water in the coolers over there, so help yourself," Bobby directed.

Jace went to one of the coolers and grabbed two beers—one for himself and one for her. Sadie quickly realized she didn't know anyone there, and it was freaking her out. This was why she hated parties. That, and her gift was a constant worry and not to mention that she felt like a fish out of water. She hated that the most because it actually made her want to run and hide.

"Hey Sadie!"

She turned around at the sound of her name and was beyond happy to finally see someone she knew.

"Hey, girl! How have you been?" Ashley asked her.

"Good. How are things going with you?"

"Great—a lot of homework, of course, but nothing to worry about. Do you know Chloe already?"

"No, not really," Sadie admitted. "I just meet her tonight."

"Well then come with me," Ashley told her. "I'll introduce you to a few of my friends."

★★★★★

"This is Erica, Amanda, and Lisa," Ashley said. "Ladies, I would like you to meet Sadie."

Sadie said hello to all the girls. She couldn't help but notice that all the girls looked different, but slightly alike in a way as well. Erica had short black hair, black eyes, and a slightly heavy body frame. Amanda had shoulder-length blonde hair, blue eyes, and a slender body frame. Lisa had long brown hair, hazel eyes, and a slightly heavier body frame. However, what made the girls look so much alike were their smiles and the positive energy they radiated with. They all seem like a cool group of girls and friends.

"Okay, girls. Let's go sit over at the beach logs and chitchat to welcome Sadie into the group properly," Ashley suggested.

★★★★★

"Hey, beautiful."

Sadie froze as she reached to grab another beer from the cooler. Adam was standing in front of her, and all she could think was, *Oh boy. I'm in trouble.*

CHAPTER 5

"Hi, Adam. What are you doing here?"

"Well ... I was invited too," he said with a smirk.

"Oh. Right. Sorry, that was rude."

Adam smiled at her as he took the beer from her hand and popped the top.

"Thanks," she said, feeling the familiar butterflies in her stomach that came from being around him.

"Do you want to take a walk by the water and talk again?" he asked.

She did, but she was having fun with Ashley and the girls too and would hate to leave them. Plus, Jace was around somewhere, and even though she really wanted to go with Adam, she wasn't sure she could do that to Jace. After all, she'd came with him.

"Sadie."

She knew that voice, and immediately froze as she turned to see Jace. He didn't look happy. Without another word, he took her by the hand.

"I was looking for you," he said.

"Yeah," she said, squeezing his hand for reassurance. In response, Jace smiled down at her.

Sadie looked over at Adam and saw he had a smirk on his face. It felt a bit like he was challenging Jace, and it made her a little uncomfortable.

"Come on, let's go," Jace said, turning and leading her away without another word to Adam.

She stopped midstep when she realizes she'd totally forgot about Ashley and her friends. "Wait, Jace. I forgot about Ashley and the girls. I really should go say something to them, or they'll think I'm rude."

"It's okay," Jace assured her. "I already talked to Ashley. That's how I knew where you were." He then continued to pull her along as they made their way down to the water.

Why is he so angry? She had to know. "Jace, what—" But before She could finish her thought, Jace pulled her to his chest and kissed her right on the mouth.

She wrapped her arms around Jace's neck as her stomach began doing somersaults. His lips were so soft and warm.

When he finally broke the kiss and stepped back, Sadie was grateful to have a moment to catch her breath, but also a little disappointed.

"Why did you do that?"

"Because I wanted to."

Jace was her best friend, and she couldn't picture her life without him, but she never thought of them being together this way. However, the kiss had been amazing and it felt like fireworks going off in her body. Sadie had never been the type of person to jump into things blindly.

What if they did this and it didn't work out? Could they still be best friends? She just didn't know, so she did what she was known for and that was she ran.

"I'm getting kind of tired, and it's been a long day. I'm going to head home."

"Yeah, sure. We can head back."

"No, go ahead and stay. I can walk back myself."

"Are you sure? I don't really like you walking back by yourself."

"Yeah, it's not that far and besides, I'm a big girl. Don't worry. Go have fun," she said with a smile that she didn't feel, but she hoped it would stop him from worrying about her.

"Okay, but can you at least text me when you get home so I know you are safe?"

"Yeah, I promise. Don't worry so much. You will get wrinkles at your young age, and all your groupies will be disappointed." Sadie let go of his hand. She was too embarrassed to look back after making such a stupid joke, but she couldn't think of anything else to say to lighten the mood.

As she walked back, she listened to the waves and wondered when life became so complicated. For a split-second, she missed her old life. She was beyond confused and overwhelmed with all these different things, and now her best friend was stepping over the line of friendship to something more. Did she want that, or did she want Adam? She wasn't sure. For now what she needed most was some rest. She'd be sleeping in her own bed alone tonight.

★★★★★

The morning light cracked through the window when Sadie opened her eyes after tossing and turning most of the night. When she arrived in Jace's room, she saw he was fast asleep, so she sat quietly by the side of his bed and shook his shoulder to wake him. Jace's eyes blinked a couple of times before they finally opened.

"Hey," she whispered.

"Hey yourself."

"Did you sleep well?"

"No, not really," he told her. "I missed my girl next to me."

She'd missed him too, but sleeping in his bed wouldn't have given her time to think clearly. "Sorry, but I couldn't be in here last night."

"Just last night?" Jace asked as he sat up in bed.

"I want to go slow. I'm still in the process of getting to know me. I have a lot on my plate right now. However, one thing I know is I can't see my life without you in it." Sadie leaned down and placed a light kiss on his warm cheek. When she looked into those sleepy eyes of his, she couldn't help but smile.

"Babe, I want to help you with that any way I can, and we can go as slow as you want—whatever makes you feel comfortable. I just want a chance to show you how much you mean to me."

She curled herself in Jace's embrace. He kissed her gently on the lips before closing his eyes. She did the same, feeling completely relaxed and glad.

★★★★★

"I wanted to go to the dealership today. Can you come with me?" Jace asked Sadie.

"Sure. I can't wait to get my pink Jeep today," she joked.

"Ha ha … very funny."

Sadie laughed as they headed to her first class, but before she could walk through the door, Jace grabbed her wrist and pulled her back and gave her a deep unyielding kiss that she felt in her whole body. When she opened her eyes and looked at his blurry expression, she saw he was smiling. Then, without another word, he turned and headed his own way.

The only thought that ran through her mind as she sat down was how she couldn't wait to kiss Jace again, since he was such a good kisser.

★★★★★

I'm going to show her everything, and she will understand that she is mine and always was from the very beginning.

Where did that come from? She looked around the courtyard and spotted three other people. There was a couple sitting at a table having lunch and a guy sitting alone by the fountain reading a book. But she wasn't even looking at any of them, so how did that thought pop into her mind?

Adam had asked her to meet him on their break, and she'd agreed. Even though Jace asked her not to talk to him anymore, she just couldn't. She felt too drawn to him, and she really hoped Jace would understand and trust her, just as she trusted him completely.

"Hey," Sadie said smiling when she saw Adam walking up to her.

"What are you doing out here all by yourself?" he asked.

"Waiting for you, of course."

"Good answer," he said as he sat across from her at the picnic table.

She laughed while admitting to herself how cute today. As Adam sat down, he looked behind him in both directions.

She couldn't help but laugh again before asking him, "What are you doing?"

"Just making sure Jace isn't going to pop up from behind me and ruin our moment."

"He's in class," Sadie assured him.

"Then my day just got even better," he said with a smirk.

"Do you have a problem with Jace?" she asked. She could still feel tension between the two guys.

"No, of course not. Jace is a great guy. I want to be just like him one day."

"Are you being sarcastic?"

"Of course not. I have nothing but admiration and respect for our beloved Jace."

The tension she felt between these two guys who didn't even know each other seemed weird. She figured it must be a guy thing, and she just didn't understand. Besides, she did tell Jace that she was getting to know herself, so he would trust her to make the right decision.

"Well, that's enough about Jace," Sadie said. "I would like to carry on with our previous conversation."

"Oh yeah?"

"You do want me to feel more comfortable so we can be friends, right?"

"Of course," Adam told her. "Ask away then." His sunglasses covered his eyes, so Sadie couldn't tell if he was being serious.

When he looked over to her and smiled, it made her feel even more comfortable to be around him, and she wanted more.

"Question?" he reminded her.

"Okay … What is your favorite thing to do?"

"That's easy. Spending time with you," he said casually.

"Seriously?"

"I was being serious, but let me see … What do I like to do? Let me think … I guess I can say I like anything that is fun or that keeps me entertain."

Why doesn't he ever give me a straight answer? she wondered.

"Okay, my turn. What is your favorite thing to do?" Adam asked.

She smiled. That was an easy question. "I love books."

"What type?"

"I love all stories, but my favorites are fantasy and, of course, romance stories. What girl doesn't love a guy who falls hopelessly in love with her?"

Sadie couldn't help but be enthusiastic when it came to explaining her favorite kind of stories. Books had always played a big part in her life, but they became even more important after her parents had passed away. When she felt alone and isolated from the world, she would turn to her books and then she wasn't alone anymore. It was like the characters in those stories became her friends and took her on amazing adventures with them.

"I'm impressed," Adam told her.

"Thanks."

"I have another question."

"I believe we have time for one more question even though I should be asking you the questions," she joked.

"Do you want to make something of your life?"

Wow, what a question, but she wouldn't tell him about her family gift—even if she did like being around him. She didn't trust him with something so private. Only Jace had her complete trust on that.

"To answer your question, yes. I want to do something important. Who wouldn't want that? But as of right now, I think it's important we head to class." Sadie said as she grabbed her bag and stood up.

"Why does time fly when I am with you?"

"Aw, that was sweet."

"What? You don't feel the same?" he said with a mock frown and a hand over his heart like she'd wounded him.

"Maybe, but I can't answer that, because we should be heading to class already."

"You can't say something like that and leave a guy hanging."

"Sorry, but that is all the time we have," she said with a laugh.

"Then how about you come out with me tonight?"

CHAPTER 6

Sadie wasn't expecting to be asked out on a date. There was definitely a connection between them, but they hardly knew each other. Although it sounded nice, she simply couldn't.

"I don't think that's a good idea," she finally answered.

"Can you tell me why you don't think it's a good idea?" Adam asked.

"I have plans with Jace tonight."

"You can't get out of them and come with me instead?"

"Well, no. He already asked, and he's my best friend. I won't flake on him."

"Okay then. How about you give me your number instead, and I can text you later? That sounds like a reasonable compromise, doesn't it?"

Will Jace be mad? she wondered. *I mean, it's not like we're a couple.*

Sadie really didn't know what they were at the moment, so she figured it shouldn't be a problem to give a friend her number.

"Okay. Give me your phone," she finally said, deciding she was going to do what she'd wanted.

★★★★★

When class was over, Sadie gathered her things together and got ready to head over to the football field when she felt Adam grab her wrist and pull her to his chest. Before she could say anything, his lips were pressed against hers.

She was really starting to enjoy the kiss when all of sudden Adam's lips were gone, and he walked away without another word.

★★★★★

"Hey," Sadie said, smiling at Jace when she finally made it to the football field.

"Hey, babe. We should almost be done. Give me another hour or so. Okay?"

"Sure. I'll read until you're done."

"That's my girl," Jace said before giving her a quick kiss on the lips as he returned to the field.

★★★★★

"Hey, Sadie."

"Hi, Ashley. What are you doing here?" Sadie asked, setting her book on her lap.

"I'm waiting on Brandon. We're going to the movies after he's done with practice. So how things with you? I didn't get to see you again at the party after Jace went looking for you."

"Things are good. I'm sorry about the party and how I disappeared without a word." Sadie still felt extremely guilty for doing that, especially after they were all so nice to her.

"It's cool. I'm guessing Jace found you and everything was all good?"

"Yeah, he did," Sadie said with a smirk as she remembered the surprised kiss Jace had given her by the water.

"The girls and I are going to get coffee tomorrow. Do you want to come?" Ashley asked.

"I would love to," Sadie agreed.

"Cool. Give me your address, and I'll swing by and pick you up in the morning."

"Okay." Sadie was beyond excited that she was doing a normal thing like going out for coffee with friends. It was like a dream come true to her, and she wasn't ashamed to admit that.

"You ready, Ashley?" Brandon called out as he Eric and Jace approached them.

"I'll see you tomorrow, Sadie," Ashley said as she laced her fingers with Brandon's.

"You bet," Sadie called out, waving goodbye to Ashley before she turned to Jace and Eric.

"Eric's going to drop us off at a dealership that he says has a great variety of different Jeeps," Jace announced.

Ever since she had known him, Jace had always talked about his first car being a Jeep.

★★★★★

The car ride felt like ten seconds, but the rest of the

car shopping experience felt like it had taken ten hours. After making their way around the dealership several times, Jace finally found the Jeep he wanted.

Finally, Sadie thought to herself. She was glad it was over because she could sum up the whole ordeal in one word: boring. Jace, on the other hand, took everything so seriously. And so, Sadie kept her mouth shut and just went along with it.

"What do you think?" Jace asked her.

"It will do," she told him. "Black isn't pink, but I'll deal. So what are the rest of the plans for tonight besides buying a Jeep?"

"I could tell you weren't exactly having fun at the dealership today."

Sadie obviously hadn't done as good a job hiding her boredom as she'd thought. She flinched and turned herself toward Jace to apologize but was surprised to see that he actually had a smile on his face.

"It's okay," he assured her. "As a reward for dragging you through all that, how about you go and make yourself a bubble bath and soak while I make dinner? We can eat outside on the beach by candlelight."

"What girl could argue with that?"

Jace held her hand the whole way up to the apartment until he unlocked the door. It was like he had to keep touching her, and it actually felt the same for her—almost like his touch filled her with warmth and happiness.

"You go relax, and I'll get everything ready. Give me an hour."

★★★★★

Sadie collapsed on bed with a cheesy grin on her face. She was looking forward to dinner, but there was still a tiny part of her that was afraid to lose Jace as her best friend and also lose the person she was becoming. She still wasn't sure on what to do.

Beep.

Sadie pulled her cell phone from her bag to check who had texted her.

Hey, beautiful.

Her stomach did somersaults. She really didn't think he was going to text her so quickly, but she couldn't help but be glad that he did.

Hi Adam, she texted back.

Thank god! She does remember me. I was starting to get worried.

Ha ha. Of course. I'm just shocked that you actually texted me is all.

Sadie got up and headed to the bathroom to turn the water on. As she added the bubble bath, she heard her text alert go off again.

You're interesting and intrigue me. So what are you doing right now?

Sadie eased herself into the tub, leaning back and letting the bubbles and hot water completely relax her before texting back. *Relaxing before dinner.*

I thought you had plans with Jace tonight? he responded.

She smiled. *I do. Our plans don't start for another hour. What are you doing tonight?*

I have some family things to take care of.

I thought you told me you weren't close with your family.

I'm not really, but when my family needs me, I'm there.

She bit her bottom lip, not sure if she should send her next text. After a few minutes of contemplation, she decided she really wanted to know. *Tell me about your family please?*

It felt like ten minutes had passed and still no response. She couldn't help but feel her heart sink, realizing he wasn't going to answer her question.

But then she finally got a response: *My mother is a strong independent woman. My father is a respectable man who always shows his best to people. And then there's my younger brother, the all perfect good man that never does anything wrong and always tries to be everyone's hero.*

Wow. That was more than she'd hoped he would share with her. It was still vague, but it was still something. She couldn't help but wonder about his little brother and what he meant about him being everybody's hero. Did they have a close relationship? There were so many questions she wanted to ask, but she didn't want to push too hard. *Thank you*, she texted back, grateful for what she got.

For what?

Finally opening up to me, she explained.

You're welcome. I'll let you get back to your plans. I'll talk to you later sweetheart.

He called her sweetheart. Where did that come from? It felt so personal and scary at the same time. High school Sadie would never have been this open and free with a guy she had just met—let alone let him kiss her.

"Hey, babe, dinner's ready," Jace called from the other side of the bathroom door.

"Okay," she called out. "I'll be right there."

She left her hair loose and put on a pair of white jean shorts and a royal-blue button-up blouse.

Jace was waiting for her by the sliding glass doors with a smile on his face. "You look gorgeous," he said as he came up to her and placed a light kiss on her lips. He then grabbed her by the hand and led her outside to the beach.

Sadie was speechless as she spotted a small wooden table, complete with a white tablecloth, on the beach. He had circled the area with paper bag lights, and on the center of the table sat a flickering white candle with pink and white roses.

"Wow, Jace," she gasped. "It's beautiful." She leaned up to give him a quick kiss on the lips, but when she pressed her lips to his, she didn't want to break away. Obviously, neither did he, as he wrapped his arms around her back and pulled her to his chest, sliding his tongue out a little to get her to open her mouth. She was happy to oblige because she wanted to taste him just as much.

After a minute, Sadie pushed him back to catch her breath. "We better eat," she suggested.

"Yeah, you're right," Jace agreed. "Go ahead and have a seat. I'll be right back with our food."

Sadie picked up the flowers and smelled them. They were beautiful, and the waves were breathtaking. She didn't know what it was, but for as long as she could remember, she had loved the water. Her dad had called her his mermaid because he swore she was part fish.

Jace came back with two plates and two water bottles. "Do you need any help?" she asked.

"Nope," he said, revealing a delicious Caesar salad.

It was topped with seasoned grilled chicken, shaved parmesan cheese, and garlic croutons.

"It looks delicious," she said while grabbing her fork to dive in.

★★★★★

After dinner, the pair took a walk on the beach.

"Do you regret giving me a chance beyond friendship?" Jace asked Sadie during their walk.

"No. I'm actually happy, and I think the real reason I wasn't sure before was because I couldn't bear the thought of losing you. You're too important to me."

Jace stopped walking, and she looked up at him, confused.

"Baby, I'll never leave you—no matter what. I told you before. You're stuck with me. I'm never leaving you. In fact, I just got a great idea for what we can do tonight."

"Oh yeah? What's that?" she asked, not sure where he was going with this.

Jace smiled at her, and before she knew it, he had scooped her up in his arms and was running to the water.

When she came up from the cold water, she couldn't help but have a look of shock directed at Jace.

"What was that for?"

"My mermaid loves the water," he said with a sexy smile.

Sadie had never told him that her dad used to call her his mermaid. She wrapped her arms around him and kissed him deeply. He smiled before giving her one more quick kiss and then leading them out of the water.

★★★★★

When they got home, Sadie changed out of her wet clothes and put on something warmer. She found Jace sitting on the couch in the living room.

"I want you to read my mind," he said to her when she sat down.

"What?" she questioned, obviously confused.

"Please, baby. Just try."

She closed her eyes and focused her mind on his. If she had to explain what she was experiencing, it felt like she was feeling around in the dark and looking for a link that would open his mind to her. It takes longer with some people than others, but everybody has it somewhere. When she finally finds it, it felt like the snap of a rubber band as her mind connected with the other mind. Sometimes it was beyond painful and sad; other times it was hopeful and filled with love and happiness. Because of that roller coaster of emotion, she didn't want this gift. She didn't want to handle other people's unknown feelings, it seem like to much and besides, how was it fair when nobody would be around to help with her feelings?

And then, just like that, she felt Jace's thoughts come to her:

This girl before me is a walking angel. She will do things in this world that will change people for the better. I'm completely in love with her. She'll never be alone again, because I'll always be there for her.

He loved her and believed in her. It was that simple. Sadie leaned over and placed a deep kiss on his lips as he wrapped his arms around her lower back and push her to lie down on the couch. She let herself feel the heat building inside of her as Jace deepened the kiss by plunging his tongue inside her mouth with strong strokes that made her breathless.

Jace broke the kiss and looked at her. "Did it work?"

"I love you too," she said, answering his unspoken question.

He flashed her the cutest smile right before placing his lips back on hers and then scooping her up in his arms to carry her down the hall. Everything was moving at light speed, but she didn't care at the moment. All that mattered to her was getting as close to Jace as possible.

Please don't let her find out the truth. I must protect her no matter what.

What was that? Sadie thought. *Is my mind still linked to Jace's? What truth is he afraid for me to know?* Sadie suddenly felt like a bucket of cold water had been dumped on her. She placed her hand on Jace's cheek. "I think we need to slow down a little."

He looked at her slightly confused before saying. "Okay, baby. How about we get in bed and watch a movie together?"

She smiled and nodded. That sounded perfect. Plus, it would give her time. Jace gave her one more quick kiss before getting out of bed to turn the light off and grab the remote.

Sadie curled up on his chest when he return and made herself comfortable—or as much as she could. She knew she should probably tell Jace what had happened and ask what he'd meant, but she was afraid to find out what it was. She never would've thought Jace had been keeping a secret from her. Why would he? Before she could think much more about it, Sadie's eyes grew heavy. She heard Jace say, "Night, baby," and then place a gentle kiss on her lips before she finally closed her eyes.

CHAPTER 7

SADIE AWOKE THE NEXT MORNING with Jace's arm wrapped around her stomach. She smiled as she ran her fingers up and down his arm, feeling the softness of his skin.

"That tickles," Jace whispered sleepily as he moved his arm to squeeze her stomach tighter.

"Good morning."

He kissed the back of her neck. "Morning, baby."

"I need to go get ready before Ashley arrives," Sadie told him.

"No. Give me five more minutes, and then I'll let you go," Jace said while nuzzling his nose into her hair and getting more comfortable.

She laughed and cuddle back in his embrace. In truth, she could use five more minutes as well. Sadie decided that she trusted Jace, so whatever this truth was that he was hiding from her, he was probably doing it for a good reason. He would tell her when the time was right. She believed that.

★★★★★

Sadie heard the knock on the door as she left her room.

"Hey, Sadie, you ready to go?" Ashley called through the front door.

"Yeah," Sadie called back.

As she tried to leave, Jace grabbed her hand and pulled her toward him. He placed his lips on hers in a deep kiss. She heard Ashley gasp in surprise, which made her smile during the kiss.

Jace broke the kiss and looked down at her with a smirk. "Go have fun with the girls."

She smiled as she stepped out of his embrace very dazed and a little unsteady on her legs. She wondered if his kisses would always affect her so much, because it was fun.

"Girl, you've got some explaining to do," Ashley said with a laugh as they walked out the front door.

Sadie just kept smiling in response. In all honesty, it felt good to be smiling and feel so happy. She hadn't felt that way in a long time.

★★★★★

Sadie and Ashley met the girls at the coffeehouse and grabbed a table where they could sit down with their drinks.

"Okay, Sadie. I've given you enough time. Let's hear it," Ashley said.

The other girls looked at her quizzically, not sure what Ashley was talking about.

"Girls, when I picked Sadie up this morning, let's just say Jace gave her one of the most perfect goodbye kisses I had ever seen," Ashley explained.

All the girls turned and looked at Sadie, hungry for more details. She laughed as they looked like a pack of wolves after their prey or something.

"Let's just say that Jace and I took our relationship to a completely different level," Sadie announced.

"When did this happen? I thought you guys were only good friends?" Ashley asked.

"Well, it kind of happened suddenly at the beach party and just took off after that." That was all she really planned to tell the girls because the kiss and everything else felt very personal. She wanted to keep it to herself.

"Is it different now that you guys live together?" Mia asked.

"No, not really, because ever since we were kids, he would sometimes come through my bedroom window and stay the night when things were hard for me so I wouldn't be alone. Jace, my sister, and her husband are the only family I have, and I'm grateful to each of them and love them dearly."

"Why is that?" Erica asked.

"When I was twelve, my parents died in a horrible car accident. I met Jace shortly after that."

All the girls extended their condolences to her. She nodded as the all-too-familiar lump of pain formed in her throat.

"Well, I think Jace and you are perfect together. I'm so happy for you." Ashley said cheerfully.

"Thanks," Sadie said gratefully as the conversation

started to turned to more lighthearted topics, such as the bunnies Ashley was looking after in her vet class and of course how cute they were with their soft, furry tails. And then there was Mia's love for clothes. It felt like the girl could talk about them for hours because she talked about fashion with such passion and enthusiasm it was kind of inspiring.

Just then, Sadie felt her pocket vibrate. She figured it was probably Jace texting, but when she pulled out her phone, she was surprised to see she'd gotten a text from Adam: *Good morning.*

Sadie managed to text back without anyone noticing. *Hey you. What's up with you today?*

Nothing much. Just wanted to see if you wanted to have lunch with me tomorrow. Say, one o'clock?

Another lunch date. Sadie really wanted to go. She liked Adam and really hoped that they could become good friends in the long run. After thinking about it for a minute, she had her answer and texted back: *Yeah sure.*

Great. You want to meet me around eleven at the beachfront café?

Okay. See you there, Sadie texted back.

Jace had said that he trusted her and respected her decision to make friends. She was finally starting to become her own person, and she wanted to embrace that and see where it went. She didn't want to lose her new confidence because of being so wrapped up in a new relationship with Jace. Since being her own person was the most important thing to her.

When she returned home from her coffee date with the girls, Jace was sitting on the couch watching television.

"Hey, babe. Did you have fun?"

"Yeah, I did actually," she said as she sat next to him. "We have plans for lunch tomorrow as well. You don't mind, do you?"

"No, it's cool. I can share you a little bit more, but after that, you're all mine for the rest of the weekend."

Sadie's heart sank a little. She never thought she could feel so low. She didn't like lying to Jace, but she didn't know what else to do. She wanted to see Adam no matter what. She really hoped she wasn't hurting anybody by her actions because she wouldn't be able to live with herself.

"Thank you for being the best person I could know," Sadie said. "I love you." She gave him a deep kiss, maybe to appease her guilt somehow.

"The only reason I'm this great guy, as you say, is because you made me that way."

★★★★★

Sadie arrived at the cafe five minutes before eleven and grabbed a table by a window. When she looked up from her seat, she was happy to see Adam walking toward her.

"Hi," she said, smiling.

"I'm glad you could make it. I have a surprise for you. I decided to tell you a little bit more about me."

"Oh yeah?" Sadie said. "Why the sudden change of heart?"

"I don't know. What I can say? I'm full of surprises," Adam noted.

"Okay. Let's hear it then. I'm all ears."

"I told you a little about my family before, but I didn't tell you the reason I left them behind. My family is like every other family. We have good times and bad, but my mother had a tragedy that happened to her when she was a child that caused her to change forever. She lost her older sister to suicide.

"My mom and my aunt were very close—practically best friends—so when my aunt died, my mother became very angry and distrustful of people. She believed her older sister could've been saved somehow, and it was the world's fault that she died."

"I'm so sorry for your loss." Sadie felt like her heart was breaking apart after hearing his words and the pain behind them.

"I appreciate that. Let's just say my mother isn't the easiest person to get close to because of that tragedy. But when my father came into her life, she began to soften up a bit, and eventually, she fell deeply in love with him. When I was born, and later my younger brother, she loved and protected us with every ounce of her soul, but she always instilled the belief in us to look out for each other and never trust anybody because the only people that care about you are your family."

"Are you and your younger brother close?" Sadie asked.

"No, not really," Adam admitted. "My younger brother doesn't see things the way our family sees them. He believes we should help all people any way we can, but a person's actions are nobody else's fault. We do what we can and hope for the best. If the worse happens all we can do is learn and adjust the best we can."

She liked his younger brother's thinking. She could

tell, that Adam didn't agree. The slight look of disgust on his face made that clear.

"What do you believe?" Sadie felt like she had to ask.

"I believe our fate is written for us, and all we can do is either live great or terrible lives like my aunt. I believe she lived her fate and followed fate's design perfectly, however I also believe there are certain people who are gifted and can change a person's fate and it's their responsibility to humanity to help out as best as they can."

"Why?" she asked, feeling a pit develop in her stomach. It felt like he was talking about her and her mother, but how could he know?

"See, I believe that people who are gifted with extraordinary abilities have certain responsibilities to people who are less fortunate. That is why they are gifted to begin with and if they don't do that, then all they are is selfish people." He spoke with such certainty almost like it was an unwritten law.

"What if these people want a normal life like everyone else?"

"Well, that is not an option, like I said that's selfish thinking."

"That hardly seems fair."

"Life's not fair, Sadie,"

"I do agree that sometimes life's not fair and the hands that we are dealt are harsh, but I don't think we should blame that on other people because they are gifted and they are not. We all have one life, and we should make it the most memorable we can. If we can help people, that's awesome but we won't know if we don't try."

"You sound like my younger brother," Adam said with a smirk.

"Does your younger brother still live with your parents?" she questioned.

"No. He just recently moved out. Of course, my mother was sad to see her baby go. Even though he didn't see things the way my mother saw them, he was always her favorite."

"So how come you are not close with your family anymore?"

"Simply, it's because of the pain and anger I saw in my mother's eyes. I couldn't take it, so I left as soon as I could to make a life of my own. However, I do plan to make the person who caused my mother such pain and loss pay for everything they have done. There is always a cause and effect to everything."

"Why would you say that?"

"Simple. I know that you are one of the gifted people I mentioned earlier."

She couldn't help but gasp in shock. *Had he said all that stuff purposely to gage her reaction?* she wondered. "Why?" she finally managed to ask.

"Why? Or do you mean how did I find out about your little secret? It was that day in class when you froze up. I knew you were gifted even though you were trying to hide it. So what is your special ability anyway?"

Sadie felt like there was a rock in her throat. No matter how hard she tried to breathe, it felt like she couldn't. What should she do? Even though he already seemed to know, it was beyond scary to actually admit it out loud—especially after all the things he'd said about gifted people's responsibility to society. She had to try and look at the positive side. Maybe if she told him, then she could help him see things in a more positive light and help him understand better. Yes. That's what she'd do—help him see the good in it. Adam was no different. It was just like helping anybody, and that meant no time for fear.

Just be strong and tell him the truth, she thought to herself. "Yes. You are right. I am gifted. I have the ability to read minds."

CHAPTER 8

WHEN SADIE ARRIVED AT THE football field, she saw
Jace talking to the other players. It was Monday,
and her weird weekend was over after telling Adam about
her gift. Adam acted differently toward her, like he was
struggling to decide what to do next and before she knew
it, he told her he had somewhere to be and just walked off
and left her. She was so lost, so she ended up just sitting
there for a while.

She never told Jace about her lunch date with Adam.
It weighed heavily on her mind, and she found herself
easily distracted the rest of the weekend. Which made her
feel even guiltier since how kind Jace was to her, doing
anything he could to make her smile. She only gave him
half her attention in return. She knew she needed to make
it up to him.

Jace looked at the bleachers and ran over as soon as
he spotted her. She smiled, wrapped her hands around
his neck, and before he could say another word, placed
her lips on his. She felt his tongue touch her bottom lip
to open her mouth, and when she did, her legs turned to

jelly. She clung to him even tighter as she melted deeper into the kiss.

"Hello," she said, breathing hard after breaking the kiss.

"Hey, we should be done in about hour. Do you mind waiting for me?" he asked.

"No. Of course not."

"Thanks, babe," he said and gave her one more quick kiss on the lips before running back to the field. She smiled and walked up to the top bleacher where she pulled out her book.

★★★★★

Sadie realized the same girl had been sitting on the bottom bleachers since she had arrived. At first, she had just glanced at her, and nothing looked out of place. It looked like she was doing some kind of homework or studying for something. She appeared fully engrossed in the textbook on her lap and had a notebook and pen on top of that. She was wearing an oversized gray sweatshirt, dark-blue jeans, and white Converse. Her hair was pulled back into a long ponytail. It was almost like the girl was trying to hide herself in her oversized clothes in a way. Sadie couldn't really explain it, but she could tell something was wrong with the girl. There was a wave of sadness washed over and consumed her.

Sadie stood up, put her book in her bag, and headed in the girl's direction. Something told her to go. The girl didn't even acknowledge her presence when she sat down. She figured it was likely because of her earbuds.

Sadie gently tapped the girl on the shoulder, and she

looked up instantly. She smiled and waved at her in a friendly way. The girl slowly removed her earbuds and looked at her skeptically.

"Hi, my name is Sadie. It's nice to meet you."

"Hello," she responded.

"Do you like football?" Sadie asked. The question sounded lame even to her ears, but she wasn't used to talking to new people. She was trying her hardest to get this girl to open up to her, so she could understand why she had such a wave of sadness around her.

"No, not really," she answered. "I was just looking for a place to get caught up with my homework."

"Oh well, I really didn't like football much before either, but since Jace taught me the game, I'm starting to enjoy it."

"Oh yeah? Who's Jace?"

"The quarterback over there," Sadie said

Jace looked over at her in that instant and gave her a half smile. She couldn't help but smile back, and just that little smile made her instantly feel better and more confident about herself.

"Can I ask you a question?" the girl asked Sadie.

"Sure. What's up?" she said, happy for any kind of communication between them.

"Why are you trying to talk to me? I'm nobody."

Sadie's heart broke hearing those words. No one should think that way. "Well, I just moved here, and it's not against the law to make new friends, right? And besides, you seem like someone who is pretty cool. So why not talk to you?" Sadie could tell that had been the right thing to say because the girl started to relax after that. "Do you mind if I ask what your name is? It will just be more comfortable to talk if we know each other's names."

There was a moment of pause on the girl's face, and Sadie worried for a moment that she wasn't going to tell her. But thankfully, the storm clouds in her eyes seemed to clear up, and she looked up at Sadie with a small smile.

"My name is Amy Wells."

"It's nice to meet you, Amy. So do you live with your family or on campus?" Sadie asked.

"I live with my mom and stepdad. And you?"

"I share an apartment on the beach with Jace."

"You live with Jace? Where is your family?" Amy asked.

"My older sister and her husband live in Yuma, Arizona. That's where we're from," Sadie explained.

"Oh, wow. Is it scary moving away from your family?"

"No, not really. I have Jace, so I never feel alone."

"Hey, babe. You ready?" Sadie looked up to see Jace at her side.

"Yeah, and this is my new friend. Amy, this is Jace."

Sadie wanted to laugh when she saw how Amy's cheeks were turning red, and a shy smile appeared on her face.

"Hi, Amy. It's nice to meet you," Jace said sweetly as he held out his hand.

"Hey," Amy whispered back as she took his hand.

"Do you have a phone, Amy?" Sadie asked. She really wanted to talk with Amy more; plus, she seemed like a nice girl who could be a good friend down the road.

"Um, yeah," she said while pulling her phone out from her back pocket and handing it to Sadie.

Sadie programmed her number in it and then sent herself a text so she'd have Amy's number as well. "It was nice meeting you, and I hope we can hang out soon," she said, handing Amy her phone back.

"Okay."

It felt great to see a happy smile on Amy's face instead of the sadness that had clouded her earlier. This whole interaction was different than the one she'd had with Jenny. It was way more serious and something she didn't want to mess up.

"See you later," Jace said to Amy as he grabbed Sadie's hand.

Amy waved goodbye to Jace. "I think someone has a crush on you," she whispered to him as they headed out.

Jace slung his arm around her and whispered in her ear. "Too bad. My eyes are only for one girl."

"I wonder who that could be," she said. She began to laugh but was interrupted when all of a sudden she was pushed up against the Jeep, and Jace's mouth was on hers.

She melted as she slowly ran her hands up Jace's arms to wrap them around his neck. He pressed himself in closer, deepening the kiss and running his tongue across her bottom lip, When Jace finally broke the kiss and looked into her eyes, she could feel his hunger for her.

"Does that answer your question about who that girl might be?" he asked in a husky voice.

Sadie smiled and nodded, giving him one more quick kiss on the lips before stepping back while he opened the door for her to hop in.

"Brandon told me about a club he is taking Ashley to tonight. Do you want to go and meet up with them?"

"Yeah, sounds like fun." She figured she'd give Amy some space that night and then try texting her the next day to see if she wanted to hang out.

★★★★★

Sadie looked at herself in the mirror after an hour of going through her entire closet. She'd finally decided on black leggings and a long black tank top with a huge cat face on the front and finished the outfit with a bunch of silver bangles on her wrist, her black leather jacket, and her black ankle boots and her hair down, wavy and causal.

"Wow, baby. You look beautiful," Jace said as his placed a sweet kiss on her lips when she met him in the living room.

"Thanks. You don't look half bad yourself," she said, looking at Jace in a gray button-down shirt and blue jeans. He did look cute in jeans.

When she looked up, Jace had a smirk on his face, which made her blush, knowing that he knew she was checking him out.

"No need to be shy, babe," he said smiling and giving her another quick kiss.

She laughed and slapped her hand on his chest to get him to stop. He chuckled as he wrapped his arm around her waist as they headed out.

★★★★★

The club had a dark wood floor, wooden tables, solid

black chairs, and a wall bar on the right, but what caught her attention were all the colors. There was a huge blue chandelier in the center of the floor with purple and blue lights bouncing all over the dance floor as the music played. Circular dark-purple couches wrapped around the dance floor. It was really pretty to look at.

Brandon and Ashley were already sitting at one of the tables closest to the dance floor. Sadie went over and gave Ashley a hug while telling her how great she looked in her red halter dress and silver sandals.

"Did you want something to drink?" Jace asked Sadie.

She nodded, and Jace leaned over and kissed her cheek before leaving for the bar with Brandon. She couldn't help but move her body to the beat of the music. It was too addicting to be ignored, and it felt extremely freeing—almost like all her worries and stresses just faded away and it was only her and the music.

When Jace and Brandon returned carrying drinks, Sadie was still bouncing up and down in her chair. Finally Ashley grabbed her hand and led her down to the middle of the dance floor as the beat of a new song started. Sadie closed her eyes and just let the music flow through her body. It was intoxicating and completely freeing. It felt like she was letting go of everything that was tying her down at the moment.

As she moved to the beat of her fourth song, she felt two strong, warm hands grab her waist from behind and pull her against a hard chest. She wasn't scared, because she knew that it was Jace. She moved her hips up against him with a wicked smile and felt his hands tighten around her waist.

His mouth came close to her ear. "Honey, you need to stop doing that. You're killing me," he said in a husky whisper.

Sadie smiled and turned around. She wrapped her arms around his neck and pulled him down to her lips. She opened her mouth to him and felt his tongue invade her mouth. It felt like her whole body was on fire, and she couldn't get enough of it.

As she opened her eyes to smile at Jace, she was surprised to see she was wrapped up in Adam's embrace, which meant she'd kissed him—not Jace. She took a step back from him and held a hand over her mouth. What had she just done?

"Too late now. I got a thorough taste of you, and I enjoyed every minute of it," Adam said before he walked away from her and blended into the crowd.

Sadie suddenly felt sick to her stomach and had to get off the dance floor as soon as possible. She didn't feel so free anymore as she hurried away, weaving in and out through the crowd, looking down at her feet. She collided into another set of arms and instantly stepped back out of fear that it was Adam again.

"Sadie?"

She knew that voice and was relieved to see Jace standing before her with a concerned look on his face. Sadie fell into Jace's embrace and accepted his warmth and comfort, feeling protected like always.

"Sadie, what's wrong? Are you okay?" he asked as he pulled her back from his embrace.

She wanted to tell him what had happened, but if she did that, it would mean also telling him she'd lied about her lunch date with Adam and that Adam knew about her gift. She was too shaken up to do that. She needed Jace more than anything right now, so she leaned up and placed her mouth on his, pouring all her love into their kiss while wrapping her arms around his neck, melting herself into his embrace.

She felt Jace wrap his arms around her lower back and squeeze her tighter as he embraced the kiss. She gladly accepted everything he had to offer in that kiss as she poured in everything she felt as well.

When Jace pulled back to gather his breath, he looked down at her. "You want to get out of here?"

She nodded. He gave her another quick kiss on the lips before grabbing her hand and leading her off the dance floor. However, as she followed Jace, she could feel something behind her or more like someone and when she turned back around, she saw Adam staring at her from a distance. He had a strong look of possession on his face, and she noticed his hands were down at his sides balled up into fists. She wanted to get away from Adam as fast as she could because she needed Jace and loved him completely. She turned her back on Adam and followed Jace out of the club with no regrets.

★★★★★

Sadie laughed when Jace pushed her up against the side of the Jeep and gave her a deep kiss while his hands ran up the underside of her breast. She felt a shiver travel through her body in response.

"I couldn't help myself. You taste so good," he said

after breaking the kiss and opening the door for her to climb in.

She couldn't hide the goofy smile on her face as she embraced the feeling of warmth in the pit of her stomach that followed.

★★★★★

The ride home seemed short, and the next thing she knew, Jace had the front door unlocked and was pulling her to his room. Of course, she was more than willing to go. When he stopped at the foot of the bed, she wasn't afraid. Instead, she put her arms around his neck and looked into his eyes.

"I love you," she told him.

Jace grabbed the hem of her shirt and pulled it up over her head. She couldn't help but shake uncontrollably when her shirt hit the floor. It was the first time she had been this personal with a guy, and it was scary to take in.

"You are so beautiful," Jace said while placing gentle kisses right below her right ear and down her neck.

Who knew a kiss right below the ear could be so pleasurable. When he reached her shoulder, he slipped her bra strap down. She closed her eyes at the feel of his fingertips on his skin, and his mouth felt so warm and good. He took his mouth from the side of her neck and planted a kiss on her lips as he unclasped her bra. Jace stepped back and slid her bra slowly down her arms all the way and dropped it to the floor and then pulled his own shirt off.

Jace wrapped his arms around the small of her back and gave her another hard, deep kiss. She couldn't help but shiver as her breasts rubbed against his bare chest, giving her a rush of pleasure that made her squeeze her legs tighter.

Jace bent and scooped her up in his arms and lay her down on the bed. "Are you sure, babe? We can stop if you are not ready," he whispered down to her.

"Yes." Sadie was beyond ready, and at the moment, she couldn't figure out why she had waited to begin with. She loved Jace and needed him to erase the feel of Adam's touch and lips from her mind and body now. She knew Jace could do it because of the love they shared.

She smiled when she saw a spark in his eyes as he went on to slowly remove her boots one at a time and then traveled up her legs until he reached the top of her pants. He hooked his thumbs on the sides of her pants and slowly pulled them down, leaving only her panties. Jace started placing small, feather like kisses on her left hip as she arched her back, grabbing handfuls of the pillow. She was turning into a hot mess of need, ready to explode at any minute.

"Jace?" she gasped.

He kissed her hard and deep before hooking his thumbs into her panties and slowly pulling them down.

"Sadie, open your eyes," Jace said sweetly.

She opened her eyes, not even realizing that she had closed them. It made her feel good seeing the look of absolute devotion for her on Jace's face as he unbuttoned his pants and slid his zipper down.

This was it. There was no turning back now as she watched him pull a condom from his wallet and open it. She could feel him at her center as he lowered himself on top of her while placing light kisses on each of her eyelids and then her forehead before finally placing a deep, hard kiss on her lips while grazing her lower lip with his teeth.

"Don't worry, baby. It will hurt only for a moment, and then it will feel a hell of a lot better. I promise," he said.

Jace continued kissing her deeply as he slid inside her until an unbearable pain shoots through her. She couldn't help but cry out. Jace placed soft, gentle kisses on her lips and neck, telling her how beautiful she was and how good she felt.

She gave Jace a squeeze on his arms to let him know that she was finally okay. He kissed her neck and slowly slid out of her and then slid back in all the way. The pain she was expecting wasn't there. Instead, a feeling of intense pleasure came, so she wrapped her arms around his neck as he continued to thrust into her. The pleasure inside her built into a tidal wave and continued rising higher and higher until it was ready to consume her completely. With one more thrust, it all came crashing down on her, and she screamed.

Jace followed her shortly after, squeezing her tightly as he groaned. Sadie was trying to catch her breath as small aftershocks traveled through her body. Finally, Jace looked up at her and smiled.

"That was amazing," he said.

Sadie just smiled as she watched him get off the bed and head to the bathroom. She couldn't have moved even if she wanted to. All her limbs felt like jelly at the moment. When Jace returned to bed, he pulled her toward his chest and threw the blanket over them.

"Are you okay?" he asked as he ran his fingers through her hair.

She snuggled closer to him, feeling amazing. "Yeah, I'm perfect," she whispered before her eyes slowly closed, and she drifted off to sleep.

★★★★★

What am I doing here again? As she looked around, she noticed the football team wasn't on the field practicing. Amy was still sitting in the same spot, and Adam was walking up to her and taking a seat next to her.

She watched as Amy smiled and laughed at everything Adam said. It appeared that they knew each other, but it was weird because all of a sudden, Amy checked her watch and hurriedly grabbed her stuff before saying a quick goodbye and running off the field with a look of fear on her face.

Sadie looked over at Adam and saw a smirk on his face as he shook his head, got up, and went in the opposite direction. The fear she'd felt earlier hearing all the things he said about gifts came back to her again as if he were standing right behind her. Was she dreaming all this because of the kiss at the club? Sadie couldn't help but have doubts about Adam. Who was he, and why did she feel this strong jealousy after seeing him with Amy?

CHAPTER 9

SADIE WOKE THE NEXT MORNING feeling more relaxed than she had ever felt before. She couldn't help but smile as last night's events replayed in her head.

"Morning, beautiful," Jace said as she felt him tighten his arm around her stomach.

She tilted her head back and looked up into his eyes. He had a content look on his face as well.

"Good morning."

"Do you feel okay?" he asked.

"Yeah, I feel great," Sadie assured him. She was sore, but it was a good kind of sore.

"Are you sure?" he asked again with a concerned look on his face. He began to look down at her body to double-check that she was okay.

"I'm not going to lie. I am sore, but I'm enjoying it because it was the best moment of my life," she said while placing a sweet kiss on the side of his cheek.

Jace gave her a deep kiss on the mouth and then scooped her up in his arms and carried her to the bathroom before setting her down in the shower. He ran his hands down her back in a soothing manner as she stepped under the hot running water. He grabbed her mandarin orange body wash and put some in his hands.

"Can I?" he asked, looking up at her.

She nodded and watched as he knelt down and put his hands at her right ankle. He then began massaging up her body. She closed her eyes, feeling his hands travel to the inside of her thighs and then to her center. She couldn't help herself and moaned in pleasure as his fingers started circling her fold. Layer after layer of pleasure filled her until she was just a ball of feelings and nothing else. When his finger pushed up in her, she couldn't take it and moaned as she shattered into a million pieces.

Jace held her by her hips as he stood up and gave her a quick kiss on the lips. "Sorry. Couldn't resist. You're so beautiful—I had to touch you again."

★★★★★

When Sadie finally made it to her room after a very long but enjoyable shower, she was surprised to see it was only about seven o'clock. It was early, but she felt so well rested and content as if she'd slept for ten hours instead of her usual five.

She grabbed a pair of jean shorts, a light-blue shirt, and her black-and-white chucks and put her hair in a nice loose, ponytail. As she went to go collect her clothes from Jace's room, she couldn't help but look at Jace's bed and feel everything they did together from last night as if moments only passed. Her belly felt warm and happy all over again. She had no regrets about what they'd done, she was completely in love with Jace.

The football field … And just like that, her dream came rushing back. Maybe her dream was one of Adam's memories, but whatever the case, she had to know what was going on.

As she dropped her dirty clothes off in her room, the greatest smell in the world came to her. Her nose followed as if it had a will of its own, and there in the kitchen was a fresh cup of coffee waiting for her on the counter. She wrapped her hands around the cup and felt the warmth travel through her body before she took a small sip, enjoying the sweet caramel taste as it traveled down her throat.

Jace chuckled.

"What?" she asked with a laugh.

"You just look so cute standing there drinking that coffee as if it were the best thing in the world."

To a girl, coffee is the best thing in the world, and to Sadie, it was number one. She put her coffee down and walked over to Jace with all the uppity attitude she could muster. "Are you making fun of my love for coffee?" she questioned.

Jace put his cup down and wrapped his arm around her waist to pull her close. "I would never do such a thing—not if I want to live."

Good answer, she thought as she laughed and rested her head on his chest. She had never felt this happy before in her life. It was like she knew herself better than she ever had before.

★★★★★

Sadie sent Amy a text during her free period to see if

she was free to go grab some coffee before her next class. No more than a minute later she got a response saying she was. Sadie felt like this was great first step; she just hoped the rest of it went just as perfectly.

As she stood by Jace's Jeep as she saw Amy walking toward her with her head down and her bag slung over her shoulder. It was a very sad picture.

"Hi," Amy whispered shyly as she approached.

"Hey, Amy," Sadie said. "You ready to go?"

"Nice wheels," Amy said as they hopped in the Jeep.

"Thanks. It's Jace's."

"Your quarterback boyfriend? What a surprise."

"Yes, that is true. But, Amy, Jace is, my best friend first and foremost," she said, hoping to clarify any misunderstanding she sensed from the snide tone in her voice.

Amy leaned her head back and closed her eyes. "Look, I'm sorry. I'm not this person. I'm just still not sure why you want to be my friend."

She needed to boost this girl's confidence by a lot. She parked in an open space at the coffeehouse and turned in her seat. "It's like I told you before. I just want to make friends is all, and you seem like a really nice girl," Sadie explained. "Come on … Let's go. I'm in the mood for a caramel Frappuccino."

★★★★★

"So what are you going to school for?" Sadie asked as she and Amy grabbed their drinks from the barista.

"I'm studying to become a teacher," Amy answered.

"Your parents must be proud. What grade are

you planning to teach?" Sadie noticed that when she mentioned her parents being proud, Amy kind of zoned out, and her eyes had this hurt look come across them.

"I want to go into second grade. Little kids need guidance and support—mostly someone to tell them they are doing a good job, because that's what my father taught me. He was a firefighter and the best there was, always working hard and giving it his all. He still had time in his day to read to me every night and tell me how proud he was of me every chance he got."

"Wow, your father sounds like an amazing man," Sadie said.

Amy glanced down at her coffee with a sad look in her eyes. "He was," she whispered.

Sadie looked at the sad girl sitting across from her and opened her mind. The heartbreak she felt was an understatement as she saw that Amy's father had passed away in a horrible fire that had started in an abandoned building. She knew this kind of pain from her own personal experience. Amy had lost a parent too soon and losing someone you love with all your heart is a crushing blow. That pain never goes away. All you can do is learn to endure it and carry on their love inside yourself.

"So what are you going to school for? I kind of got us sidetracked telling you my reasons for my goal," Amy asked, smiling.

Sadie could tell by her mannerisms she was probably trying to change the subject. She had done that many times in the past when things got too tough or painful for her. It was easier to just brush it aside and focus on something else.

"I have always loved books, so I've always wanted to be a writer. I want to be able to write my own stories to share with people," Sadie told her.

"Oh yeah? Who are some of your favorite authors?"

Sadie couldn't help but laugh. That would be a really long list, but she could name a few of her favorites. "Abbi Glines, Suzanne Collins, Jessica Lemmon, J. K. Rowling, Stephanie Meyer …"

"I take it you must read a lot."

"Yeah, it is a bit of an addiction for me. I always believe as long as you have a good book, it can take you to unimaginable places and make you feel good about yourself."

"I feel the same way about music," Amy said. "A good song always makes me forget all my worries, and it's cool having someone be able to relate to how you feel at the moment."

"If you don't mind me asking, how do you feel?" Sadie finally asked. "It's just … You seem to have this wave of sadness about you."

Amy held her head down again, but this time something had changed. It was like she wasn't so tense this time and could relax a little. "My father died saving someone from a fire."

"I'm so sorry, Amy."

"I'm not, because my father was an awesome man who did what he loved most of all. I know deep in my heart that my father had no regrets in the end, because he was doing what he always was meant to do. If I become bitter or angry because he left me, that would dishonor his memory and what he stood for. I don't want to do that to him, because I loved him too much."

"Wow, that's truly inspiring," Sadie told her. "How is your mother? Is she as strong as you are?"

Amy's eyes change from sadness to anger in a second, and the relaxed pose she had earlier went to very tense and agitated. "No. My mother is not strong. She is as weak as they come," Amy snapped. "All she cares about is making her new husband happy and completely forgetting about my dad and me."

Sadie gasped quietly as she read Amy's mind again and saw her stepfather and how angry he got at her the morning when she didn't have his breakfast ready. He shoved her into the counter and caused all the ingredients she had out to fall on the floor, making a big mess. Sadie could see that afterward when Amy lifted her shirt up in her bedroom there was a huge bruise in the center of her back from the counter. Nobody deserved that from a family member, blood related or not.

★★★★★

Adam was already sitting down when Sadie entered the classroom. She told herself it didn't matter as she took her seat because all she had to do was pay attention to the professor and then leave for the day. She could do this because she loved Jace. Adam didn't scare her, and she'd prove it.

"Hey, Adam," she said.

"Hello there, and what have you been up to lately?" he asked with a cocky smirk on his face.

Sadie couldn't help but pause and wonder if he knew

about her going for coffee with Amy. It was starting to get a little creepy—him knowing where she was and what she was doing. She wondered what his deal was.

"Nothing much. What about you?"

"I'm just sitting here thinking you have not learned anything from our little conversation."

"Excuse me?" Sadie asked. *What was he talking about?* she thought to herself.

"Let me ask you something again. Do you think a person should suffer consequences for interfering with things they shouldn't be involved with?"

"I'm not sure I know what you mean."

"Obviously you weren't paying attention before, so I'll say it again," he said coldly. "Fate has a design for each person, and no person should mess with it or willing to suffer some kind of consequences. They can't go half in on something that important."

"I don't believe that's true," Sadie noted. "If I can help them and change their fate for the better, then why shouldn't I? By doing that, I help everyone involved."

Adam didn't say anything after that, and even when class was over, all he did was mumble a goodbye to her and left without looking back at her.

★★★★★

"Hi," Laura said, answering the phone.

When Sadie had gotten home, the first thing she'd done was call Laura. She needed her big sister. "Hey, Sis," she said. "I need some advice."

"I can feel you've got something big to tell me, so spill it."

Sadie started with the beach party and how Jace at one moment was being the Jace she knew all her life and then the next moment he was giving her the best kiss of her life. She also told Laura on how confused she felt afterward and the fear that ran through her head of losing Jace and the friendship she'd built with him over time.

"I'm not surprised, to be honest," Laura said.

"Really?" Sadie was kind of shocked by Laura's reaction. Had she missed something?

"Yeah, of course. There always was a noticeable connection between you two. Jace always looked at you as if you were made for him, but the real question I have for you is how do you feel about him?"

Sadie felt totally clueless if her sister knew all that already. *It's about time to change that*, she thought. "Jace completes me and makes me feel strong. I think I have always loved him as my best friend, but now it feels like a different kind of love is growing between us. When he is around and kisses me, my stomach feels like it is full of butterflies."

"You are definitely hooked," Laura said with a laugh.

"Was it like that with Luke?"

"Of course. It felt like I had found the other half of my soul."

"It feels like such a scary, powerful feeling," Sadie noted.

"Yeah, it is," Laura agreed. "But you know what? It's the best feeling."

"Yeah, I agree, Sis ... However there is something else I need to talk to you about, though."

"What's that?" Laura asked.

"Well today, I used my gift on a girl on campus, and it worked perfectly. It was super small, but it was still something and a big step for me." All she got was complete silence on the other in of the line, and it worried her that Laura was mad somehow.

"Sadie, please be careful. Are you sure you are ready for something like that? You just started enjoying your new life. I would hate for anything to ruin that," Laura said with deep concern.

"Well I feel it is my responsibility as our mother's daughter to honor her by helping people like she did, and I also believe that she would want me to try. Don't worry, Sis. I'll be careful. I always am." As Sadie said the words, she couldn't help but remember the dream she'd had about their mother. She knew in her soul that she was doing the right thing.

"I don't know, It's so dangerous, and I don't want anything bad to happen to you. You're the only sister I have, and I love you dearly."

"I love you too, but I know it's the right thing, which brings me to why I called you. I met a girl just recently who seems to be in real pain, and I can't turn my back on her now. I need some advice from my big sister."

In the end, Laura just told her to try to be there to help Amy as much as she could. Laura really did believe that Sadie was doing the right thing and couldn't turn her back on Amy now. Of course, before they ended their phone call, Laura did stress for her to be careful and call her no matter what. She didn't want any secrets between them.

Unfortunately, Sadie did still have one secret she was

keeping from Laura—Jace too. She felt guilty, but she didn't know what else to do. Adam became such a big secret that it felt like there was no turning back. It seemed impossible to tell the truth to the people she loved most.

★★★★★

Sadie had just washed the last dish from dinner when she felt Jace right behind her, his lips touching the shell of her ear.

"Did I tell you how beautiful you look today?" he asked as he continued placing light kisses behind her ear.

"Nope, but it is always nice to hear," she said with a smile as she leaned back into his chest. Sadie felt him tug on her waist to turn her around, and he instantly placed his lips on hers without another word. She wrapped her arms around his neck and felt his hands slip to the upper part of her thighs, pulling her up to wrap her legs around his hips as he carried her to the bedroom and set her down on the edge of the bed before slowly beginning to undress her.

His fingers ran over her naked skin, which gave her electric shocks throughout her body as he placed his lips on hers to open her mouth as his tongue slid into her mouth and tasted her. It felt so good all she wanted was more.

"Aren't you tired from practice?" she asked when he finally broke the kiss and gave her some much-needed air. She really was hoping that he wasn't tired at all.

Jace smirked at her. "Do I feel tired?" he said as he rubbed up against her.

She could felt his hardness through his jeans and

couldn't help but feel excitement bubble up in her. Sadie placed her hands on his chest and pushed down so Jace was resting on his elbows on the bed as she straddled his hips. She grabbed the hem of his shirt and tugged it off. She placed a deep kiss on his lips as his hands came around her hips and squeeze her.

Sadie could feel his stare and sexy smile on her as she unbuttoned his jeans and moved them down along with his boxers. She ran her hand over him and felt how incredibly strong he was. She lowered her head and kissed the crown of his penis, and he instantly lifted his hips, trying to push himself into her mouth as his head relax on the pillow while his hips move up so she could take more of him in.

She smiled, knowing she could bring him such great pleasure. Plus, he tasted so good filling her mouth. Sadie felt him lace his fingers in her hair and give her head a gentle push down as she took more of him in. His hand gripped her hair tighter, so she went faster and could feel his orgasm coming.

Afterward, she couldn't help but smile. "That was fun. I want to do that again."

Jace laughed and then flipped her on her back with a grin. "As much as that sounds like fun, I have a better idea."

In the end, she had to admit his idea was even better as he slowly began to make love to her.

CHAPTER 10

THE BEEPING WOULDN'T STOP. ALL Sadie wanted was five more minutes of sleep. She opened her eyes grudgingly as her phone was beeping like an alarm clock by going off every five minutes. She could feel Jace was asleep with his arm around her and just a sheet covering them. After what they'd done the night before, she could probably drop a plate, and he wouldn't wake up.

Beep.

There went her phone again. Someone was really trying to reach her. She slowly slid out of Jace's embrace, grabbed his shirt from the floor, and tiptoed to her shorts to get her phone. She couldn't believe her eyes as she saw she had ten text messages already, and they were only five minutes apart sometimes less.

Sadie??

The messages were from Amy, one after another.

Can we talk?

Please answer.

I really need someone to talk to.

You said I could talk to you.

Something was wrong. She could feel it in the pit of her stomach, but Laura said all she could do was listen because telling Amy about her gift would be a bit overwhelming and Amy would think the worst and maybe never talk to her again.

Sadie took a deep breath before responding. *Hi, I'm here. Is everything ok?*

It's just that … I'm feeling kind of low and didn't want to be alone right now.

Why, what's wrong? Sadie responded.

Just the usual family drama that consumes every day of my life. I didn't clean the house and have dinner ready for them so my stepfather got really angry with me, and then my mom got mad at me for causing such a scene. Sometimes I feel like such a disappointment and failure for making my mom upset.

Sadie felt bad for Amy's home situation. She quietly left the bedroom and answered the text: *You should think better of yourself. I know we just met, but I can tell you are a pretty cool girl and love your mom deeply. That comes across. I know it does.*

It was around one o'clock in the morning when she finally asked Amy if she wanted to meet for lunch at the campus café so they could talk even more.

★★★★★

When she went back to Jace's bedroom, she was surprised to see Jace sitting at his desk with his laptop open. He looked up at her at the doorway.

"Is everything okay, babe?"

"I thought you were sound asleep."

"I can't sleep without you next to me."

"That was Amy, There is something I haven't told you about her. When I first saw her, I felt this huge wave of sadness coming from her, so I went down and said hello to her, hoping I could figure out what was wrong.

"Her stepfather is abusing her and treating her like trash. Then her own mother only seems to care about pleasing her new husband and not her own biological child. Amy's biological father was a good man and a great firefighter who died saving people's lives. I can tell she really looks up to her father and respected him, so it's extremely hard on her with her mother's new husband constantly taking out his anger on her and telling her she won't measure up to anything."

Sadie could see Jace had developed a heated look on his face after hearing what she had to say. "That's shit," he said. "Her stepfather sounds like a real asshole."

"Yeah, I agree. Amy is a pretty cool girl, actually. I think we can be great friends. I really want to help her out."

"How are you going to help her without telling her about your gift?"

"I already talked to Laura about that, and she told me the best thing I could do for the time being is just be there as a friend and listen. We are going to lunch tomorrow, and I'm going to be there for her to listen, offering support anything I can do.

"I hope everything goes well, and you can help her, babe."

"Yeah so do I, but now I have a serious question for you," She said with a wicked grin. "What are you doing right now?"

"Just finishing an assignment. Why what's up?"

Sadie smile and took off her shirt and threw it in Jace's face. "I was going to take a shower and was wondering if you cared to join me," she said over her shoulder with a laugh.

"Hell yeah," Jace said, hurrying off and scooping her up in his arms while heading off to the bathroom.

★★★★★

Sadie sat in bed next to a sound asleep Jace as she worked to finish up some of her homework. All of sudden she felt her phone vibrate. She had put it on silent to avoid waking Jace, so she keep it close in case Amy texted her again.

Hello :)

The message was from Adam. She was surprised and wondered what he could possibly want after the way he'd acted in class earlier with her.

Her phone vibrated again. *What are you doing?*

Just doing some studying. And you?

Thinking about you, of course.

What she felt a mix of emotions and couldn't help but look at Jace. He completed her soul and was always there for her when she needed him the most; Jace made her feel confident and strong and, most of all, desirable and She really didn't like the person she was becoming around Adam kept secrets from her loved ones.

Thank you, but what else are you doing? She texted back, hoping to change the subject to something that she was more comfortable with.

Just hanging out with people, but I kept thinking about you and wanted to talk with you instead. Why? Something wrong?

No nothing is wrong, she wrote back. That was wrong to say, she was so confused, but she wasn't going to tell him how she really felt until she figured it out herself.

Well it looks like you don't want to talk so I'll let you go, beautiful. I'll see you tomorrow. We can talk then. I'll be looking forward to it.

She put her phone down as her head was swimming with thoughts and emotions. She felt Jace wrap his arm around her hip and place his hand flat on her stomach, giving her a sweet kiss on the cheek before getting settled back to sleep. She loved Jace, but why was she thinking about Adam and seeing him tomorrow? What was wrong with her?

"I love you," she whispered while placing a light kiss on Jace's lips.

"I love you too, baby," he whispered back to her sleepily.

★★★★★

Sadie took a table by the window with her deli sandwich and water when she notice Amy walk in and Amy wasn't alone. Adam was with her.

What's going on? She notice that Adam wasn't looking at Amy even though he was holding her hand as they walked up to the table. Instead, he was looking at her.

"Hi," she said as they reached the table.

"Hey, Sadie," Adam said with a smirk before turning to Amy. "I've got lunch, babe. Go ahead and spend time with Sadie," he said right before kissing Amy on the cheek as he made his way to the cashier.

What the hell was that? Why is Adam calling Amy baby, and why did he kiss her on the cheek? Her emotions were screaming at her, demanding answers. "How are you feeling?" she asked instead.

"A lot better," Amy told her. "I talked to Adam, and he helped me to see things differently … Oh yeah, you never mentioned you knew my boyfriend, Sadie."

Boyfriend? What is Amy saying, and how long has this been going on? "Yeah, he and I share a class together. He has been friendly to me since I'm new and just moved here and all."

"Yeah, that sounds like him. That's what I love about him the most. He is such a great person."

"How long have you and Adam been together?"

"We just met three months ago, and let me tell you, we can talk forever about all sort of things. It never gets boring. Plus, it's so much fun to be around him."

"That's great," Sadie said with a brave smile, but she felt like she was going to throw up in her mouth. It almost felt like jealousy was eating her up on the inside. She felt sick to her stomach as she realized she'd shared a kiss with someone else's boyfriend. She was such a horrible person.

Adam returned with sandwiches, chips, and a couple of sodas. "So what did I miss?" he asked.

Her stomach twisted even more. There was no way she could eat lunch now.

"Nothing much—just girl talk, really," Amy told him.

"So Sadie, how are you and your beloved Jace doing?"

Adam asked with a smile while he popped a chip in his mouth.

"Great, thanks for asking," she said, hoping to make it clear to Adam—and herself, in a way—that she was with Jace. That wouldn't change even if her feelings were all twisted up and confused.

Adam looked at her lips and smiled before throwing another chip in his mouth. She couldn't help but feel guilt for what she had done, and everything felt even worse with Amy sitting right across from her.

"That's wonderful. I'm happy for you guys," Amy said as she bit into her own sandwich.

All Sadie could do was smile at Amy in acknowledgement.

"So, did you tell Amy here about your special gift that lets you help people in their time of need?" Sadie looked at Adam. It felt like he slapped her across the face. *Why is he doing this to me? What is he hoping will happen?*

"What gift?" Amy asked.

Adam looked at Sadie, waiting for her to answer Amy's question. She tried pleading with him to stop, but all he did was lift his eyebrows, as if to say, *Well, if you won't do it, then I will.*

"Well, you see, babe, Sadie says she has this special ability to read people's minds, and in doing that, she has committed herself to helping people in their time of need … or something like that. Is that how you put it, Sadie?"

"You can't be serious," Amy said with a look of amusement plastered on her face as she turned to Sadie.

"He is joking, right? It's not possible to read people's minds."

Should I tell Amy the truth or lie? What is the right thing to do? Damn it. Thanks to Adam, it was about to get ugly.

It was better to be up-front and honest because at least Amy would still trust her if she didn't lie about it.

Adam was trying to prove his point about not helping others because his family got hurt, and she wasn't going to let him do that.

"No, he's not joking. I really do have the ability to read people's minds," Sadie finally said.

Amy's look went from amusement to confusion in that moment. "That's impossible."

"Not necessarily, babe. I believe there is a reason why Sadie here greeted you and wanted to become your friend. I think you are one of her cases of trying to help people," Adam said.

Amy looked at her, waiting for some kind of response. If Sadie admitted what Adam had said, Amy would go back to thinking that she was nothing and believe she never wanted to be her friend. Adam was fighting dirty and that wasn't fair because Amy was nice and fun to be around. She didn't want to lose the friendship they were building.

"No. It's like I said in the car to you, Amy. I'm new to town and wanted to make friends," Sadie said.

CHAPTER 11

❝ WELL, BABE," ADAM CUT IN. "Sadie and I are going to head to our last class, so I'll see you later tonight."

"Yeah, okay," Amy said smiling and wave them goodbye.

Sadie couldn't help but feel like a failure. The whole lunch had fallen apart thanks to Adam and after she cleared up Amy's misunderstanding about their friendship, everything became awkward. She could tell Amy just assumed that the gift Adam mention was just a loose statement—nothing more.

"Hey, wait up," Adam called to her as he ran to catch up. "What's wrong with you?" he asked.

"Nothing, I'm just heading to class."

"Are you sure?"

Sadie could feel him looking at her. Can I ask you a question?"

"Of course. What's up?" he said with a slight laugh.

She could feel herself becoming angry at his laugh. It felt like he was making fun of her. "Why did you do tell Amy about me?"

"Simple. It's an amazing gift that you shouldn't keep hidden, right? You told me it was to help people, so don't be selfish and hide. Instead, be upfront and own it. Besides, I want to see if you can work miracles, because in truth, I don't believe you can, and I don't think you should pick and choose lucky winners for these supposed miracles."

"Do you know Amy well?"

"Yeah, of course," Adam told her. "Oh, wait. Are you asking about her issues with her stepfather?"

Sadie stopped walking and looked at Adam in shock. "You know about that?"

"Of course. She is my girlfriend, smart one," he said with a laugh like it was dumb of her to ask him that.

"So you're not concerned about her well-being or the way her stepfather is treating her then?"

"No, and here's why: she is a grown girl and needs to stand up for herself. Like I said before, it's her life. She needs to deal with the pain and figure out a solution on her own."

"How can you say that after knowing how he treats her? Don't you care about her and the pain she is enduring?"

"Of course I care about her, but I'm her boyfriend, not her caregiver. It's her life, and she has to change it if she wants to. My aunt just gave up and didn't even fight. If, as my mother said, someone could've saved her with some blessed powers similar to yours, then the outcome would've been different. Personally, I'm not so sure myself. However, here's the question I have for you: Why does Amy get to be saved, while my aunt didn't?

What's so different? They both have similar problems, so answer me Sadie. Why one over the other?"

She didn't know what she could say that would sound right. He had a point. What happened to his aunt was a tragedy that probably could've been prevented. So how was it fair to save Amy now? She only had one answer.

"Simple it's because I'm here, and I don't plan to turn my back on Amy. I will save her no matter what. I wasn't around at the time of your aunt, but if I had been, I would've tried to help her too. All I can say is I'm sorry for such a terrible loss."

"It's easy to say that, and correct me if I'm wrong, but you weren't Joan of Arc to the innocents until just recently," Adam pointed out. "If I'm right, all you wanted was a normal life like anybody else, and that would involve not helping anybody and being selfish with this supposed gift of yours but that is different now since all of sudden you had a change of heart, people like Jenny and Amy are the lucky winners, but that girl at the store and my aunt suffered. So, like I asked before, why does one person get help in life and not the other? How come one person follows the grand design of her fate, but the other has outside help to change hers?"

How does he know about the girl at the store? Was he there? What is going on? Sadie's mind began racing. *Is this really Adam, the guy who made me feel confident and beautiful and who I couldn't wait to be around? What if something horrible happened to Amy? He was her boyfriend. Shouldn't he be helping her?*

"You are right to a point; I'll help her and I won't run. She needs to stand up for herself and accept what life has given her. If she doesn't like it, then she can change it with her own free will. If something terrible happens to her, then so be it, because it was just meant to be." Adam said.

Sadie felt like the wind had been knocked out of her. His statement was so cold, practically heartless. What was worse was that she still liked him even after hearing all those awful things coming from his mouth. She was ashamed of herself in a way.

"Class has already started, and we're late because of this great debate—which I won." Adam said as he headed off without another word.

★★★★★

Okay, this is frustrating, Sadie thought. After making three wrong turns and an hour of driving, the gods had mercy on her soul since she finally found Amy's house.

She couldn't stop thinking about what Adam had told her before class and how wrong he was. There was no way she was just going to sit on the sidelines out of fear of what he said.

Which brings her to Amy's house and it was impressive. It looked like it came straight out of a home-and-garden magazine. She knocked on the door and an older-looking man answered the door and what caught Sadie attention most of all were his serious-looking eyes. He looked almost angry.

"Hello," he said. "What do you want?"

"Is Amy home?"

The man gave Sadie a once-over. In a way, it made her feel belittled, and it had just been a simple look.

"Amy!!" the man called out.

When Amy came to the door, she had a surprised look on her face. "Um … Hi, Sadie. What are you doing here?"

"I just came by to say hi. Is there a way we can talk?"

Amy looked at her stepfather nervously, almost like she was waiting for some kind of approval.

"Make it quick," he said. "I won't wait for dinner forever. You know that."

Amy nodded and led Sadie to the porch swing, closing the front door behind them. "I wish you would've texted first because I'm really busy right now and can't be long."

"Sorry. I just wanted to come over and see how you were doing. We didn't have a chance to really talk during lunch today."

"Okay. What's up?" Amy asked.

"Well, I'm worried about you. Nobody should hear the things you hear like being told you're not smart enough or called a failure repeatedly and be kicking around like nothing."

Amy was really quiet and stared at Sadie for a while before speaking. "Sadie, I never told you anything, so how do you know all that?"

"Well you see Adam wasn't lying at lunch when he told you about my gift. My family has carried this ability for generations," Sadie explained. "I can read the mind of anybody who is close to me and feel their deepest thoughts. When I first saw you, I felt a wave of sadness consuming you, so I read into your mind at the coffeehouse and I saw the torment your stepfather is putting you through and how alone and sad you feel from it and it broke my heart."

Amy slowly got up from the porch swing. "This is

crazy and impossible. Adam must have told you about my parents. There is no other way you would know ... You need to leave right now. I don't want to hear anymore nonsense and I don't have time for this."

"Amy, I'm just trying to help. Please just listen to me for a second."

"Well you are not helping, and I want you to go," Amy snapped.

After that, Amy just walked back inside her house and shut the front door right in Sadie's face. She could feel her eyes begin to water. This was what she always feared would come of telling people about her gift, and it felt even worse than she thought possible.

Sadie walked to her car in defeat when she heard her phone ringing. Jenny's number was showing up on her caller ID. Sadie figured she must have good news to report. Jenny must have gotten the internship at the museum in New York. She could use some good news, so she pressed the answer button on her phone.

"Hey, Jenny," she said. "It's good to hear from you. I'm guessing congratulation are in order for passing your test, right?"

"Yeah. Hi, Sadie. Well, I did pass my exam, and thank you again for helping me. But for some unexplained reason, I lost the internship. It was given to someone else."

"What?! That's terrible, Jenny! I'm so sorry. What are you going to do now?" Sadie asked.

"It's okay," Jenny said. "Yes, it's heartbreaking. I really did have my heart set on going there, but I'll just have to apply elsewhere. In fact, I'm looking right now as we speak, so I'll be okay. I will not give up on my dream no matter what."

She wished she had Jenny's positivism but so far her day had been awful, filled with one bit of bad news after another. Getting off the phone with Jenny, she realized she hadn't actually helped anybody. Sadie couldn't help but wonder what was wrong with her. How could she fix this?

CHAPTER 12

"Sadie?"

She looked up and saw Jace standing off to her right. She didn't know how long she had been sitting on the beach. All she would remembered was that when she got home, the tears would not stop flowing down her cheeks, so she had been watching the waves ever since. She gave Jace a small smile of greeting.

"Baby, what's wrong?" Jace asked as he sat next to her and wipe her tears off her cheeks.

She end up telling Jace everything through her tears about what happened at Amy's house and also about Jenny's phone call. Jace wrapped her arms around her and pulled her onto his lap. He ran his hands up and down her arms, trying to calm her down.

"Baby, I'm very sorry. Amy doesn't realize how special you are and how lucky she is to have someone like you to care for her. I think everything will work out in the end, so try not to worry."

She buried herself further in him and cried harder as he wrapped his arms tighter around her.

"My mom must be so disappointed in me. Our gift should have gone to Laura; she would have dealt with this better. I'm nothing but a failure," she said in a choked voice as she tried to hold back her tears.

"Look at me, baby. Please," Jace pleaded.

"Your mom would never be disappointed in you, and you want to know why? Because you are the strongest, kindest person I've known. You always cared more about everyone around you than yourself. Even when things were hard for you, you never let it bring you down, so I know for a fact your family gift went to the right person.

I don't want to hear any more negative things coming out of your mouth. Do you hear me? You're better than that."

She looked down and closed her eyes as Jace placed a sweet kiss on her forehead.

"Did you eat, baby?" he asked.

She shook her head no. She had to admit that she was hungry now that she was actually paying attention to her stomach.

"Are you in the mood for some hamburgers?"

"Yeah, as long as you're the one grilling," she told him.

"Of course. Am I not the grill master here?"

She laugh as she thought about how Luke and Jace always argued over who was the better grill master when they had barbecues in the backyard. Jace still believed that he'd won on their last barbecue, because Laura and Sadie had mentioned they liked his burger and after Jace heard that, he started yelling that he was the grill master as he walked all over the backyard. They all laughed.

"There is the smile I love so much," Jace said, looking down at her.

"Okay, grill master, you go get the grill ready, and I'll get everything else."

Jace leaned down and gave her a quick kiss and then pulled her up with him as they head inside.

★★★★★

Twenty minutes later, Sadie handed Jace a plate of four seasoned patties all ready for the grill. "Here you go, grill master."

"Best burgers you will ever have. You just wait and see," Jace said, grabbing the patties and heading out to the grill.

"You are so confident, However you might have new competition now that we live in San Diego. Who knows, there might be a ton of grill masters here," She said as she followed him out to the grill.

"Oh yeah? Well then I guess I will have to convince you that I'm the best."

"What do you have in mind?" she asked, even though she already had a pretty good idea where he was going with this.

"I have many different ways," he said.

"You might not get to prove that if you keep burning our dinner,"

Jace smiled at her before wrapping his arm around her waist and giving her a quick, hard, deep kiss. "Glad to see you're getting back to normal, baby."

She laughed as she watched him turn and start to flip the burgers.

★★★★★★

Dinner was great, and she felt a lot better after eating. Who could beat good burgers and homemade seasoned fries?

It's time for dessert, she thought as she went the bathroom where Jace was taking a shower. She took off all her clothes and pulled back the curtain.

Jace stared at her as she entered the shower. She stood on her tiptoes and planted her mouth on his. As she deepened the kiss, he placed his hands on her hips and squeezed her closer to him. She liked how he always made her feel strong and confident and, most important, loved beyond belief. Jace was an incredible person, and it was time to show him how much he really meant to her.

She grabbed the bar of soap and lathered up her hands. She started by lathering his shoulders and then moved down his chest. She could feel his breathing start to go faster as she worked her way down. She couldn't help but smile.

He smirked at her as he brought her closer, but she put her hands on his chest and pushed him back. She knew if she gave in to him she would lose focus, and right now, it was all about Jace.

When he was completely soaped up, she stepped back. "All done. Now it's time to rinse off," she said with a smile.

Jace grinned, and before she knew it, he had pulled her to his chest and went under the shower with her. She laughed as she wrapped her arms around his neck.

★★★★★

Jace dropped their towels on the floor, then scooped her up in his arms, and carried her to bed. She placed soft kisses all along his jawline as he set her down on the bed. She couldn't hide the smile on her face as Jace crawled up her body, placing tiny kisses on her stomach and then along her ribs, which made her squirm in delight. When he got up to her mouth, he kissed her as he slid inside her, making her whimper from feeling him all around and inside her.

She put her hands on his chest and pushed up, which broke the kiss, so she could speak. "I just wanted to tell you that you make me feel beautiful, and you make a great burger also."

Jace tilted his head back and laughed before kissing her on the lips and then buried his face in her neck. "I love you too," he whispered.

Sadie wrapped her arms around his neck and held on to him as the pleasure built inside her with each thrust.

★★★★★

"You listen to me. Sadie is my girl, and I will do anything and everything I have to in order to protect her, so I'm warning you to back off now."

She slowly opened her eyes and looked for Jace. She felt a dip in the bed as an arm came around her waist pulling her in.

"Where did you go?" she asked sleepy.

"Nowhere, baby. I have been here with you all along. Go back to sleep," he said as he kissed her cheek and settled back into bed. It felt so good being in his arms that she closed her eyes instantly and drifted back into a peaceful sleep.

★★★★★

The next morning Jace walked Sadie to class. It was like he was still worried that she might be off from yesterday even though she told him a couple of times she was all right. Even so, he stayed as long as possible, holding her hand and letting her know she had his warmth and support.

She really wasn't excited about being at school. She wanted to hide at home with a bucket of cookie dough and a couple of good books. Sadly, she knew that wasn't the way to handle things, so she turned to Jace with a fake smile and hoped it was believable.

"No worries. I've got this," she told him. "You have your own class to get to anyway, so I'll see you later."

"Nothing matters more than you do," he responded.

Sadie couldn't help but smile. He always had a way with words. "Okay, Mr. Romantic, get to class. I'll see you at the game tonight," she said, playfully pushing him away to make him go to his class. Instead of leaving, he grabbed her hands and pulled her toward him, crushing her lips to his. She melted right into his embrace, and when Jace broke the kiss, it left her breathless, almost like smoke was coming off her lips.

"Have a good day, babe."

Sadie just nodded in response and gave him one more kiss goodbye before heading into her first class.

★★★★★

As she sat on one of the sofas in the back of the library on her lunch break, Sadie thought about how slowly the day had gone. If only she had her mother's courage and confidence inside her instead of the feeling of unbelievable fear and self-doubt she had instead. She really needed to change that, or she would never be able to help anybody and her family gift would be wasted in the end. She didn't want to disappoint her mother's memory that way.

"Hey, Sadie."

She looked up and noticed Mia standing in front of her.

"Hey, Sadie," she said again. "What are you doing here all by yourself?"

"Nothing, just on my break. What about you?"

"I'm just looking for a particular book," Mia said with an exhausted look in her eyes and a heavy sigh.

Sadie could see that Mia looked stressed. There were practically bags under her eyes, and she looked like she hadn't slept for a week.

"Are you okay?" Sadie asked. "How's the fashion designing going?"

"It's going good … well, I hope so, at least. I've been working on a couple of designs for a big showcase in a month, but I'm still not sure about entering it yet," Mia said quietly

"I'm sure they are great. I can already tell you have a real love for fashion when you talked to me at the party that night. I don't think you have anything to worry about."

"Thanks, but you're just being nice since you haven't seen any of them," Mia said with a casual laugh.

"Well, if you don't believe me, I'm willing to look at them and give you my honest option if you want."

"I really don't like showing them to anyone," Mia said, looking down at her hands.

"Yeah, but you will have to show them at the showcase. You could show me, and I won't tell anyone if you don't want me to. But I honestly think they'll be great."

Mia bit her bottom lip. "Do you want t come over this weekend?"

"Sure," Sadie agreed.

"Saturday morning around ten o'clock. I'll text you my address."

"Okay," Sadie said. "I'll see you there."

"Well, I'm going to go and look for the book I need before my break is over. You coming to the game tonight?"

"Jace wouldn't let me miss it for the world," Sadie said smiling.

"Great. I'll see you there." Mia said as she headed out.

Sadie had to admit she felt a lot better about herself after talking with Mia.

"Helping out another friend? You are such a sweet girl."

Amy standing off to the side with her arms crossed and glaring at her.

"Amy … How are you? I was—"

"I wonder what she'll say when she realizes you're crazy and that you can supposedly read people's mind. You think she'll still be your friend afterward?"

She was hurt that Amy thought so little of her just so she can make cruel jokes. She'd tried to be honest friend, and in turn, everything fell apart. She could feel her eyes to begin to water so she excuses herself and walked out of the library without looking back.

★★★★★

When her break was finally over, Sadie began walking to her last class alone hoping noting bad happen on the way there and suddenly, her stomach dropped when she saw them. That had to be the reason Adam and Amy were making out at the front door of her next class.

Honestly, could life be any crueler? she thought.

Sadie took all the uneasy feelings that were stirring up inside, pushed them deep down, and started walking to the door, hoping beyond hope to go unnoticed. Adam broke the kiss the second she hit the door and looked right at her.

"Hi, Sadie."

She felt like her throat felt like it was full of sawdust. Amy looked at her with hatred-filled eyes that scorned her where she stood. She just nodded to both of them and tried to move through the door.

"Don't talk to her," Amy said. "Her craziness might rub off on you."

She sagged in defeat after hearing Amy's mean words. The girl was out for her blood, and it hurt more and more every time. Adam had a smirk on his face as if he'd taught her some sort of lesson.

"Is there a problem here?"

Sadie froze for a second. When she turned around, she was surprised to see Jace walking up to her. She couldn't help but automatically walk into his embrace and his warmth; it felt so good and safe.

Jace wrapped his arms around her and gave her a reassuring squeeze. "Well," he repeated, "Is there a problem here?"

Jace was talking not only to Adam, but to Amy as well. Sadie couldn't help but feel sad, because this all started with her trying to help Amy, and now everything was wrong. She now understood what her mom meant when she told Laura that you had to be careful when you mess with people's lives, and there could be consequences if not done correctly. She really had messed this up royally.

"All is good here. Nothing to be angry about, Jace," Adam said .

Amy remained completely quiet, just leaning into Adam the whole time. She stared up at Jace with wounded puppy dog eyes because of the tone he was using with her.

"What are you doing here?" Sadie whispered to his ear.

Jace didn't say anything but led her off to the side of the building. "The team is excused from their last class to get some more practice in before the big game tonight, and I wanted to see you." He place his hands on either side of her face and gave her a slow, gentle kiss that deepened when his tongue swiped her lower lip. She opened her mouth, feeling his warmth and taste engulf her.

"I'm glad to see you," she whispered back after breaking the kiss.

"Good," he said. "It was worth it just to get another kiss from you. See you tonight."

She smiled and nodded as he gave her one last quick kiss before turning around and heading in the direction of the football field. She really didn't know how Jace always knew when she needed him the most, but she was glad he had been there.

When she made it in the classroom, she saw Adam had taken his seat. He didn't say a word to her, which she was grateful for. She didn't have anything to say to him anyway.

★★★★★

The one good thing today was that she could honestly say she actually learned something in class. She already had a full page of notes, and for once, Jace wouldn't have to break everything down so she could understand. Now all that was left was to go get ready for the game.

"Sadie, wait."

She looked over and saw Adam's eyes right on her and his hand around her wrist, and then all of a sudden just like that she wasn't in the classroom anymore. Instead, her mind opened up to two boys in a park together. One had to be twelve years old, and the other looked to be no more six years old. They were playing together on some kind of jungle gym, and they looked so happy together.

"Sadie, did you hear me?"

She shook her head and looked at Adam again. She was back in the classroom, and she could feel Adam had taken his hand off her wrist.

"I'm sorry, did you say something?" she asked.

"Yeah. I asked if we could talk."

She wasn't sure if she wanted to talk with him anymore. So far, all their talks had ended badly.

"About what?" she finally asked.

"How about your gift and when you are going to stop messing with people's lives?"

CHAPTER 13

SADIE FELT EXTREMELY COLD AND vulnerable. On instinct, she began to rub her hands up and down her arms to create some kind of warmth inside her.

"What are you talking about?" she questioned.

"Oh, I think you know. You trying to help Amy with your little gift when I already asked you why she is so special compared to my aunt or the girl at the grocery store you left behind. You still haven't answered, and that tells me you don't have anything to say that will cancel out my point."

"Why are you so determined to make everybody suffer when we can change that and help the people around us? You know about my gift and what I can do, but instead of helping me, it feels like you're always standing in front of me and trying to block me."

"Why should I help you when you didn't help my aunt or, more precisely, your mother didn't?"

"What are you talking about?" She questioned, stunned.

"You'll know soon enough, but unfortunately, not

now. I have somewhere I have to be, so I'll see you later, sweetheart," Adam said as the back of his hand graze her left cheek while he made his way to the door.

"Adam, wait," she said, grabbing his wrist. As she did, Sadie experienced a flash of a vision:

"Honey, do you see that?"

"I'm not sure, but it looks like a boy. Let's pull over and see."

Sadie couldn't believe what she was seeing. It was her mom and dad. But why would Adam have a memory of them? Who was this guy?

Suddenly, she heard Adam's voice again. "Sadie?"

She blinked her eyes a couple of times and realized she was still standing behind Adam with her hand around his wrist. *What just happened? How am I able to read his mind … his memories … without doing anything?*

"I'm sorry," Sadie responded. "What did you say?"

"I said is there anything else you need, because you're making me late by holding my wrist like that, If you want to be close to me, all you had to do is ask."

Sadie quickly let go of his wrist and stepped back. "Sorry. My mind was wandering. I'll see you later." She had no time to argue with him or ask him how he knew her parents. She was really confused about where the memories had come from?

★★★★★

Jace was awesome, a total force to be reckoned with.

His team was winning, largely thanks to him. After the whole thing with Adam, she only had time to work on her homework a little, and she had to get ready for the game shortly after.

Ashley, Mia, and Lisa were already sitting on the top bleachers when she arrived, so they called out for her to join them. Adam was sitting farther down with a couple guys on another set of bleachers, and her thoughts drifted to her parents again. She really wanted to call Laura and tell her what had happened.

"Hey, Sadie. Are you and Jace going to the after-game party at Evan's place?" Ashley asked.

"Well, Jace hasn't mentioned it, but we most likely will." She'd rather spend the night with Jace alone, but she knew he would want to go, especially since it looked like they were going to win the game because of him. It wouldn't be right to ask him to skip it.

Sadie felt her phone vibrate in her back pocket and saw a text from Adam. It read: *Nice game. Meet me in the den of Evan's family room.*

Why? she texted back.

I know you want answers, and I'll give you whatever you want since I'm such a nice guy.

★★★★★

She was lost in her thoughts and didn't even see Jace come up to her until his lips were on her mouth and he was tugging her bottom lip into his mouth. She placed her hands on his shoulders and returned the kiss.

"Hey, you," he said after breaking the kiss.

She couldn't help but smile. "My lips are going to be swollen from all this kisses you keep taking."

"Your lips are even sexier when they are swollen," Jace said. He then gave her one more quick, hard kiss before pulling away from her.

She laughed. "So are we going to Evan's party?"

"Ashley told you, huh? Do you want to go? If not, we can do something else."

"No, I want to go, and you should go since you won the game. It will be fun." Of course, that wasn't her only reason for wanting to go, but she kept that to herself.

★★★★★

The party was packed wall to wall with people. Sadie and the girls took one of the couches, while Jace and the guys went to the kitchen. Adam had entered the house earlier with two guys, and his eyes zeroed in on her the like he could sense she was looking at him. He gave her a quick smile and then moved farther into the house.

Sadie only lasted thirty more minutes half listening to what the girls were saying before she just couldn't take it anymore. All she could think about was Adam and the answers he said he would have for her. She knew it was a bad idea, but she couldn't ignore it after seeing her parents. She had to know more, so she excused herself from the girls, saying she needed to use the bathroom. She felt bad doing this behind Jace's back, but it had to do with her parents, and she had to know more. It was too important to her.

As she entered the den, she saw Adam leaning against

the wall on the far side of the room. He looked up and smiled at her as she walked in.

"Hey, beautiful,"

"Amy didn't come with you tonight?" she asked while looking around the room.

"Nope. Her parents are upset with her again, and like the good little daughter she is, she stays and takes it obediently. So you get me all to yourself. Aren't you happy? Because I am," Adam said casually.

Sadie couldn't help but grind her teeth in frustration. "You're not concerned about Amy at all?" she asked.

"She is a big girl and can take care of it herself."

"Why are you doing this, Adam? What do you want from me?"

"Simple. I want to show you the truth, and then you'll understand how wrong you are and how up till now everything that happened was because of a choice your mother made," Adam said as he walked up to her.

She never expected him to say something like that. "What?"

"I have no secrets."

Sadie's head was telling her to move as Adam approached, but her body didn't want to move. It was almost as if her body craved to be near him, regardless of the fact that he was a jerk to her at times.

"Honey, he looks very cold."

"I know. I wonder what he's doing out here alone."

"Look, honey. He's starting to wake up."

"Hey there, little guy. Can you tell us your name?"

"Jace."

"What are you doing out here all alone, sweetheart?"

"I'm not alone. My big brother is playing hide-and-go-seek with me, but I guess I feel asleep while I was hiding. Have you seen him?"

"What is your brother's name?"

"Adam."

She felt her legs go out as she fell to the floor. Jace had known her parents, and even worse, Adam, the guy she'd met on campus and had an unexplained connection to, was Jace's older brother. *How did I not know this? Is everything in my life a lie?* Sadie felt an uncontrollable tremble start through her body that she couldn't stop.

The sound of Adam's voice snapped her out of her daze. "Sadie? Can you hear me?!"

"You're brothers." Those two words took so much energy to say because it felt like her mouth didn't want to form the words. Some part of her knew that if she actually said it, she would have to admit the truth.

"Yep. The do-gooder brother I had mentioned to you before was none other than your beloved Jace."

"I don't understand what is going on." *Why did Jace hide this from me? Does our friendship mean nothing?*

"I see by the look on your face that you're thinking the worst of my kid brother, and as much as I enjoy seeing him get knocked down off his pedestal, this whole situation isn't entirely his fault."

"What do you mean? Whose fault is what?" Sadie could hear her own voice cracking. She was barely holding it together, afraid of what he was going to say. Whatever it was, she was sure it would cause her to crumble into pieces.

Adam knelt down in front of her and looked into her eyes, giving her a small smile. "Go ask Jace, and when you want to know more, then come back to see me."

She felt Adam in every part of her body. It almost felt like she was being pulled to him. "Why are you doing this to me?" she whispered.

"I'm not doing anything. What you are feeling is the strong chemistry between us. Let me ask you a question, and let's see if you have an answer for me. Are you sure you are with the right brother? Because your body is telling me something different."

She gasped, feeling the warm and all-too-familiar heat building in her stomach. She put her hands on Adam's chest and pushed back with all her strength and she slapped him across the face right before heading out the door.

When Sadie entered the kitchen, Jace saw her and the distraught look on her face. He put his beer down on the counter and went to her instantly.

"What's wrong?" he asked as he cupped the side of her face.

She instantly became sad, as his touch wasn't soothing her like usual. She stepped back out of his reach and faced the truth.

"I know," she said.

Jace looked confused, as if he didn't know what she

was talking about. That only made her blood boil even more. He was still lying to her even after she'd told him she knew.

"I know about Adam being your older brother. How could you not tell me? Is that why you came into my life? Why you didn't want me to befriend Adam either?" she asked angrily. So many questions were going through her head that her hands were starting to shake. She needed answers.

"Sadie, please calm down. Let's go home and talk about this."

She really just wanted to walk away and be left alone by everybody, but she saw the fear in Jace's eyes, and her heart ached because of it. She knew at that moment that she couldn't walk away from him even if she wanted to, because no matter how bad he'd hurt her, she still loved him enough to hear what he had to say. She nodded and saw the tension leave Jace instantly as he started to place his hand on the small of her back and lead her to the front door. She tensed up when he came near her, so he lowered his hand. He looked as if someone had sucker punched him in the gut.

"Hey, everything okay?" Mia asked as she came up behind Sadie.

"Yeah, I'm just tired, so Jace and I are heading home, but I'll see you Saturday."

Mia grabbed her wrist and pulled her off to the side. "Are you sure you're okay? Because Jace is watching you like you are going to disappear at any moment."

Sadie looked over her shoulder. Jace was looking right at her. She felt like telling Mia what was going on, but it wasn't anybody else's business, instead, she lied. "Everything is fine. Nothing to worry about."

"Okay," Mia said. "I guess I'll see you later then."

"Yeah. Please tell Ashley and Lisa goodbye for me."

Sadie walked past Jace. she could see the hurt in his eyes. Why had he hidden the truth from her? The worst part about this whole thing was she felt like a joke, and that hurt, especially after everything they had shared recently.

★★★★★

The ride home was the longest, most uncomfortable thing she'd ever done. To have to sit next to Jace without being able to touch him or talk to him was beyond painful. It felt like someone had ripped her heart out of her chest and left the empty shell of a person behind. She'd never felt as alone as she did in that moment. She was trying desperately not to cry, but the pain was unbearable, so the tears rolled down her face quietly with no chance of stopping.

"Baby, please don't cry. It kills me to see you cry. I'll explain everything to you, and remember that I love you very much. I know everything will be okay in the end. Please just trust me."

She listened to his words, and it hurt. So when they finally arrived home, she didn't wait for Jace. She got out of the Jeep, let herself in, and headed straight for the sliding glass doors that looked out at the ocean. The water always calmed her in times of crisis, and she really needed that. She was terrified of what she was about to hear, but because it was so dark, she could hardly see anything. She just stood and listened to the waves.

She heard the front door close, and automatically crossed her arms over her chest in defense as she continued to look outside.

"Okay," she said. "Let's hear it."

She felt Jace behind her and could even hear him when he took a deep breath. It was like the room was suddenly closing in on them, and it just made her feel even more afraid.

"It's true Adam is my older brother, and I did meet your parents years ago. Adam and I had been out playing hide-and-go-seek for hours one day, I was hiding and my eyes became very heavy, so I decided to lie down until he found me. I guess I ended up falling asleep, because the next thing I knew, I woke up and was looking up at your mom. Your mom was sweet and loving and had this angelic glow about her that made me feel happy and protected all at the same time."

The tears continued to roll down her face as she listened to Jace talk so sweetly about her mom. It made her remember how she used to lay her head in her mother's lap and close her eyes while she ran her fingers through her hair. She could always feel her mother's love for her from the top of her head to the bottom of her feet.

Sadie could feel that Jace wanted to come over and hold her, but instead, he made himself remain where he stood so he could continue his story. "Adam came shortly after your parents showed up. Because it was so late, your parents insisted on giving us a ride home, and that was it. I never saw them again."

"But why keep it a secret?" she asked, still not understanding that. In truth part of her was actually happy Jace had gotten to meet her parents and see what good people they were.

"You were so heartbroken after your parents died, and even now when you think of your parents, I can see the sadness and pain that comes. I didn't want to upset you more, so I thought the best action I could take was being there for you instead and protecting you from any future heartbreak if I could."

"But you lied to me about Adam. You knew from the very beginning that I was talking to your brother, and you didn't say anything. Is that why you didn't want me to befriend him? You were afraid your lie would come to the surface?"

"I wasn't trying to hide anything from you, Sadie. I just didn't want you around my brother or my family for your own safety,"

"What are you talking about?" she asked.

"My family is different than me."

Sadie remembered Adam talking about the tragedy of what happened to their aunt. "Does this have to do with your aunt?" she asked.

Jace gave a quiet, disbelieving laugh before saying. "I see Adam has been talking, but I doubt he has told you the complete truth. Sadie, my mother has always been painfully shy and awkward; she never made friends easily, so my aunt was my mom's best friend as they grew up. They were inseparable. It was always them against the world until my aunt took her own life one day. After that, my mother became angry at herself and most of the world.

You know, I think my dad does love my mom dearly, but I also believe he feels sorry for her because she lost her sister at such a young age and how hard it was on her. So as time went on, my mother became more closed off and isolated from everyone except my father. My old man is a strong and extremely patient, he became the only person who was ever able to break through to my mother. He treated her like a queen and made her realize she wasn't alone anymore. I had a great deal of respect for him because he taught me how to truly love and care for a woman or that's what I thought when I was little."

"Had?" Sadie asked as she turned around to face him. It sounded to her like he didn't have respect for his father now.

Jace looked at the couch and then looked back at her. "Can we sit? This is a very long story, and I'd rather we sit. Plus, it will help my nerves. I hate seeing you standing there looking at me like you have to protect yourself."

She nodded and sat at end of the couch, letting some of the tension leave her body. Jace sat at the other end of the couch. It was killing her to see the space between them. A huge part of her wanted to curl up next to him and feel his warmth, but she couldn't do it right now if she wanted to get the answers she needed.

"When Adam and I were kids, our mother was always there for us no matter what. She became our best friend, as well as our mother. We had some great times, always laughing and having fun, but as we got older, our mother started to change. She became overly protected. I believe it was because Adam's and my worlds were growing as we grew up, and she wanted to protect us from the outside world. She always believed the world failed to protect her sister, so she was going to do anything possible to make sure the world didn't fail her children.

"She taught us that people were cruel and selfish and only care for themselves. And she instilled in us the idea that the only people we could depend on were family.

She believed certain people were born with extraordinary gifts that could help people, but she told us she learned the hard way that those people were also selfish and failed to save my aunt when she needed it the most. My mother never forgave the world for that."

"What was your aunt's name?" Sadie asked, pain in her voice.

It finally hit her. The whole time she had known Jace he'd never spoken of his family. He used to tell her they were busy or that he had more fun staying at her place with her sister and Luke. She never pushed the issue, because she was just so happy to be with him. Now she wished she had.

"Sara Holland," he whispered.

Sadie closed her eyes as the world she had known was crushed in front of her.

"This is all because of a choice my mother made. You didn't come into my life because of me."

She didn't think she could cry anymore, but she was wrong. She couldn't lose Jace even though everything she thought she knew was a lie. She was embarrassed to admit that felt like nothing compared to her fear of being alone.

"Please believe me, Jace," Sadie began, "My mother regretted not helping your aunt. She regretted it so much that she devoted her life to helping others and made sure that sadness like what happened to your aunt would never happen again. I'm so sorry, but please tell me … Were you ever really my friend? I need you. I don't want to be alone again," she whispered.

Jace's arms were around her before she knew it. She really wanted to push him away, but her body had other ideas, and she instantly melted into his embrace.

"Baby, stop. I'm not going anywhere. You are the most beautiful thing in the world to me, and all I wanted to do was protect you no matter what. You were always mine, and I will cherish you until my last breath. I truly love you with all my soul. Nothing will ever change that."

Jace's words went straight to her heart. Sadie pulled back and looked up into his eyes. She saw sadness as he wiped away her tears. She felt his hands go behind her neck before he slowly lowered his mouth to hers.

She didn't want to pull away. Instead, she grabbed a handful of his shirt and brought his mouth down to hers, as he gave her a deep, wet kiss that made her toes curl. Jace's hands move down her back until they reached her upper thighs and gave her a gentle squeeze as she wrapped her arms around his neck and her legs around his hips.

★★★★★

When they reached the bedroom, Jace lowered her down, and she could see the question in his eyes. Was this okay, or should he stop now? She didn't want him to stop; in fact, she needed this more now than ever, so she nodded for him to continue.

"You are beautiful, and I'm going to take my time to show you," Jace said. He gave her a kiss on her forehead and on each eyelid, and then he slowly made love to her and showed her how important she was to him.

★★★★★

She should have been sleeping after what she and Jace had shared, but her mind wouldn't shut off. Instead, she layed her head on his chest and listened to his heart beat as he slept soundly and replayed his words over and over again in her head: "The first time I knew I had fallen in love with you was the first summer vacation we spent together on the beach. I had gone looking for you one morning and couldn't find you anywhere in the condo, so I went to the beach and found you sitting next to the waves reading a book. A bright red ball rolled to your ankle, and when you looked over, there was a little girl running over to you with a goofy grin. She looked to be no more than three years old, so instead of just giving the ball back to the little girl, you smiled at her and set your book down to roll the ball back and forth with her. The little girl laughed, and you looked so happy and laughed right along with her. That's when I knew I had fallen in love with you and would love you for the rest of my life. You are not selfish; in fact, you are the most caring and open person I know, and no matter what happens, I'm going to always be with you."

She remembered how Jace had once shown up at her bedroom window and saw tears running down her face while she held a photo of her mom and dad. He said nothing and just held her and let her know she wasn't alone anymore.

Then there was one of her favorite memories when

they went to the theater, and it was Jace's turn to pick the movie. He picked his favorite—a horror movie. She hated horror movies; they scared the crap out of her, but she tried so hard to be brave for him and suck it up. However, Jace did the sweetest thing ever by holding her hand during the movie and making stupid jokes the whole time to make sure she wasn't scared. It was the best horror movie she'd ever seen because all she did was laugh the whole time with her best friend.

She leaned over and gave Jace a soft kiss on the neck. He tightened his arms around her lower back and opened his eyes.

"Baby?" Jace said.

"I love you," she whispered back.

Jace instantly relaxed and kissed her on the forehead and held her close for the rest of the night.

CHAPTER 14

"Hey, right on time," Mia said while stepping to the side so Sadie could enter.

"Hi, You have a beautiful house."

"Thanks," Mia said, closing the door behind her.

Sadie shouldn't have been surprised, but even the inside of the house was stunning. The living room had a beach theme to it with cream-colored walls, white couches, and a glass coffee table and end tables. The walls had different ocean pictures on them that really completed the room.

A woman came from the kitchen, and Sadie was struck by how much she looked like an older version of Mia. She had the same flowing light-brown hair and hazel eyes.

"Sadie, this is my mom, Blaire."

"Hello," Sadie said. "You have a lovely home."

"Thank you, dear. You girls enjoy yourselves," Mia's mom said as she exited the kitchen headed to the front door.

"Bye, Mom. Say hi to Dad for me," Mia called out as the front door closed behind her mother.

There were sketches everywhere in Mia's room plus a desk off the side that was piled high with fashion design books, sketchbooks, charcoal pencils, and what looked like a million different colored pencils. In another corner there was a table holding roll after roll of different fabrics and all kinds of tools from a sewing machine to fabric measuring tape. Plus nearby stood a dress form to pin fabric on as well.

"I certainly see you are dedicated to your dream," Sadie said as she took a seat on the bench at the foot of the bed.

"I have always loved clothes since I was a kid. When I was little, I used to love to dress up my dolls and run little fashion shows,"

"Well this looks awesome. I can't wait to see your sketches."

She could see Mia became nervous as she went to her desk and pulled out a black sketchbook from a drawer. "They're still kind of rough," Mia said nervously as she handed her the sketchbook.

★★★★★

The sketches weren't rough at all. In fact, they were fantastic. Sadie already had favorites: one was an ankle-length, two-layer red-and-orange sundress with spaghetti straps, and the other was an elegant midthigh, one-shoulder off-pink dress with a ruffle across the chest and a slim jeweled black belt at the waist.

"These are my favorites by far, but the whole collection is stunning. You are an amazing talent."

Mia looked down at her sketches and then looked over at Sadie, seeming unsure of what she'd just heard.

"They're great," Sadie repeated as she handed Mia back the sketches. "Honestly. Let's get you ready to win that showcase."

★★★★★

Three hours had passed when they finally called it a day. Sadie had to admit it was really cool that Mia valued her opinion so much.

"Thanks for everything, It was fun, and I feel a lot better about things now."

"No worries, but I have to tell you … I have a new favorite," Sadie said, pointing to the sketch Mia just finish. It was a flowing blue gypsy skirt with a thick brown leather wraparound belt paired with a thin, short-sleeved ivory sweater shirt and a long turquoise necklace and silver bronze heels. There was even a second option for the top—a black tank top with a neon-pink necklace and a thin black-and-silver belt with black heels laced with pink trim.

"Yeah, me too. I can't wait to put it together. Want to see the two dresses from earlier?" Mia asked.

"Of course. I would love to see them."

The red-and-orange sundress looked exactly like the sketch. The fabric was so soft; She thought it felt like she was touching a fluffy cloud. She couldn't help but wonder what it would feel like on her body.

★★★★★

"So how did everything go with Mia today?" Jace asked as he sat next to Sadie on the couch and pulled her close to him.

She smiled before answering. "It went really great. Mia is very talented, and her clothes and sketches are fantastic."

Jace placed his palm against her cheek and leaned in to plant a sweet kiss on her lips. She was so happy in that moment.

★★★★★

Sadie heard the knock on the front door, she put her book down on the coffee table. Jace had left to go get their dinner from Panda Express about thirty minutes earlier, so when she opened, Adam was the last person she expected to see.

"Sadie, we need to talk," Adam said.

"No we don't." She didn't want to be anywhere near him, but she didn't even make it even halfway inside before Adam grabbed her wrist from the door and pushed her back so he could move inside before closing the door behind him.

"What the hell are you doing?"

"I want to talk. There is no crime in that," Adam said, pulling her closer.

"Let me go!" She try to jerk her wrist from his grip, but she just felt his hand tighten more.

"Jace already told me everything, so I don't want to talk to you. Leave … now."

Adam instantly let her wrist go. "So you know," he said with a smirk.

"Why?" she whispered, taking a couple of steps back as she rubbed her wrist.

"Why did I get stuck with Jace as a younger brother? I have been asking that question ever since my parents brought him home," Adam said dryly.

"That's not what I meant. Why didn't you tell me Jace and you were brothers?"

"Why didn't Jace? Plus, you never gave me the chance since you were so wrapped up in my little brother."

"It doesn't even matter what you say, because Jace told me everything. You can leave now."

"Isn't that sweet? My little brother is such a good guy, always protecting you ever since you were a little girl who would cry in her bedroom over something she had no control over," Adam said dryly as he slowly walked toward her.

She felt her body completely freeze. Jace told her he hadn't told his family anything about her. So how did Adam know that?

"You think my little brother was the only one who noticed you back then?" Adam said, now standing only an inch away from her face.

She held her breath while putting her hands on his chest to push him back, but that warm feeling started again in her belly. She couldn't help but melt in his embrace and close her eyes. What was wrong with her? Her mind drifted to Jace and how he'd held her on the beach as she cried. This was wrong, so she pushed Adam back with everything she got.

"It's too bad you are the daughter of a woman who didn't bother to help a girl in her time of need but instead was only worried about herself. What a selfish, self-centered person she was," Adam whispered in her ear while placing his palm on her cheek.

How dare he talk about my mother like that? "You don't know anything about my mom, and you have no right to talk about her." She pushed him harder.

"Oh yeah? Well the same can be said about you. Did your mother know anything about my aunt or even bother to take the time to try?"

Sadie was about to tell Adam to leave when the front door opened and Jace walked inside.

"What the hell are you doing here, Adam?" Jace asked as he slammed the door and set the food on the kitchen counter before standing in between Sadie and his brother.

"Hey, little brother. I came by to check on Sadie. She didn't seem to well at the party when we were talking, so I was concern," Adam said sarcastically.

"You can go. Sadie is mine, so she is no concern of yours,"

"Oh, little brother, you might think she is yours, but let me ask you something. Did you ever stop to think about our mother's feelings? Or even care at all?"

Jace's back stiffening for an instant before answering. "Of course I care about our mother's feelings, but Sadie had nothing to do with what happened to our aunt. She was in a dark place from what mom told us, and even if Sadie's mom had tried to help her, there was still a chance it wouldn't have worked and she couldn't have saved Aunt

Sara. Other people shouldn't have to pay for such a terrible tragedy. It's not their burden to bear."

She couldn't just stand there anymore. She had to say something. "I'm sorry about your aunt, but all my mom wanted was a normal life like everybody else. She didn't ask for this gift, and at the time, she made a horrible mistake. But she worked hard afterward to help as many people as she could in your aunt's name as a way of trying to make amends. That should count for something." How could one choice affect so many lives? Fate can be beyond terrible at times.

Jace grabbed Adam by his shirt and shoved him back to the front door. "Enough, Adam. You need to leave now."

She cringed when Adam's back slammed into the front door. She grabbed Jace's other arm to stop him. She couldn't bear to see Jace fight with his brother. Suddenly, everything went away.

"I know who you have been hanging around with, little brother," a younger Adam was saying to a younger Jace.

"Adam, you don't know anything."

"Sure I do. She is the daughter of that woman who ruined our family. Mom should know who you decide to include in your life."

"Sadie has nothing to do with that. You don't know her."

"Do you even care about our mother? You know that family needs to pay for the pain they caused our family."

"No they don't."

"What are you saying?"

"I am saying is that what happened to Aunt Sara was horrible, and I'm very sorry Mom had to suffer through that, but, it isn't anybody's fault. It was a horrible tragedy that fell on Aunt Sara and that's all."

"My sister may have been in a terrible place, and I was too blind to see it. My failing to save her is a burden I will carry with me forever. However, there should've been someone who could have saved her. Those supposed walking angels with talent and abilities who could do God's work. When my sister needed an angel more than anything, they were too self-absorbed to save her. Now tell me, boys, whose fault is it for my sister and your aunt's death? The aunt who would have loved to have met you and watch you two grow up to the young proud men you will become."

Jace and Adam immediately stopped arguing and turned to their mother who was looking at both boys with a disappointed look on her face.

Jace turned back to his brother. "You're an asshole, Adam."

"What? I didn't do anything. Mom just reminded you what is important which is your family above all else, not some scared little girl you feel sorry for."

"You are completely wrong, Adam, and I will show both of you just how wrong you guys are."

Sadie stumbled backward and lost her grip on Jace's arm.

"Sadie, are you okay?" he asked with concern as he held her in his arms.

She looked up at Jace and realize she was sitting on the

floor cuddled up in his embrace. She couldn't remember how she ended up on the floor to begin with.

"Yeah," she whispered as she let her head fall against Jace's chest.

"What happened?" Adam asked, leaning down with a curious look.

She cuddled into Jace's chest more, hoping he would understand her message to get Adam to leave.

"You need to leave, Adam, and I'm not going to tell you again"

"All right, little brother. I get the point. I'll see myself out."

She could feel Adam take one more look at her before leaving, and an uncontrollable shiver traveled through her body. Why was she so attracted to him?

"Baby, talk to me. Please," Jace said after they heard the front door close.

"Do you agree with your family that my mom is at fault for your aunt's death?"

"No, of course not. My mom told me once that my aunt really never opened to anyone, and even my grandparents had practically ignored her and focused on my mother more. They believed they could raise my mother the way they wanted and in the image of a successful and financially secure daughter they had always wanted. I guess when my grandparents had my aunt, they weren't really ready to be parents but dealt with everything the best they could.

"When my mother came along, she tried to include my aunt in everything she did, and over time, they became the best of friends. However there was still a loneliness in my aunt's heart, and I think it had a lot to do with my grandparents never really stepping up and being good parents to her. I wish I had gotten a chance to meet my aunt, but that's not how it worked out. It's not your mother's fault, and it's not your fault."

Sadie only felt a little bit better hearing that. She couldn't help but think how it would be different if her mom had helped Jace's aunt that day at school. Would she still be standing here completely in love with Jace? She really didn't know.

★★★★★

Sadie sighed as she opened her eyes again. It felt like her mind was running a million miles an hour with so many what-ifs. She was starting to have a killer headache.

She felt Jace's arm tighten around her waist, and she close her eyes and try to relax and let sleep take her away.

★★★★★

"Sadie?"

She turned around and saw Adam leaning against the wall in her living room. *What's going on?* She looked around for Jace.

"What are you doing here again?" She asked him.

"I'm here because you want me to be here," he said with a chuckle.

"What?"

He chuckled again. "You know what I'm talking about—that warm feeling that travels through your body when you see me or when I touch you. You can't deny it. I can see it in your eyes now."

She didn't want to admit that she did feel something for him and was scared because she didn't understand why. "I love Jace. I want to be with him forever." Maybe if she said it enough times, it would kill the feelings she had for Adam.

"You might think so, and maybe a part of you does, but I know deep down you are also curious about me and what you feel," Adam said with a mischievous smile.

He had to be wrong, but no matter how hard she tried, the words wouldn't come out of her mouth. Instead, she like her stomach was filled with butterflies. She closed her eyes in reaction to the heat that came from his touch. It felt like a sizzling fire traveling through her skin, and her eyes become hazy with lust. She couldn't stop thinking how much she wanted him to kiss her.

"I love you. I have always loved you."

She opened her eyes as Jace's words filled her mind and stepped back from Adam's grasp, shaken. "I love Jace, so this thing—or whatever it is that was between us or anybody else is not worth it," she said, taking another step back while pushing him away.

Adam smiled and lowered his arms down to his sides. "Keep telling yourself that, sweetheart. I can wait because eventually the unknown between us will be too much for you. I'll be there when you come back to me."

★★★★★

Sadie could feel that Jace wasn't in bed with her when she opened her eyes. The sun was breaking through the curtains. She must have slept through the night finally, but after the dream she'd had, she had to admit there was something between her and Adam. She couldn't explain it, but it was like a fire that drew her to him, and no matter how hot it was, she just wanted to get closer and closer to it.

"Hey, baby."

Sadie looked and saw Jace walk into the room with a huge smile.

"Morning," she said, scrambling out of bed and wrapping her arms around his neck. She gently pulled his mouth down toward hers as she walked backward until the back of her knees hit the bed where she carelessly fell backward on the bed with a smile.

Jace broke the kiss and looked down at her. "Well, good morning to you too."

She smiled before turning to put Jace on his back as she went back to kiss him on the lips again. She grabbed the hem of his shirt and pulled it up so she could run her hands over his stomach. She heard him whisper in a strangled voice. "Baby?" His hands gripped her hips tighter. He was so good to her, and it only made her love him more, so in response, she deepened her kiss even more and got another groan out of him. Before she knew it, she was on her back while Jace was lowering onto her.

Sadie could feel his hand roam up her shirt until it cupped her right breast, and an instant rush of pleasure washed over her, turning their good morning to one of the best mornings she'd ever had.

CHAPTER 15

SADIE HAD TO ADMIT SHE was beyond lost as she looked out the window of the coffee shop. The whole Amy thing was really bothering her. That poor girl was suffering for no reason.

She had to figure out a different way to reach her, but she didn't know how. Plus, there were so many questions still floating through her mind: *Is this really the life I want? To help people all the time and take all their pain on myself? Can I even pull it off?* Her family and Jace believe she could do it, but she still didn't believe it herself.

Mia's name flashed on Sadie's screen as her phone started to ring. Sadie knew her fashion show was in two weeks, and they had been texting back forth about it for a while. Mia was excited and more confident than ever that she was going to nail the show, which made Sadie feel great

"Hey, Mia, What's going on?"

"Oh my god, Sadie. The dresses have been ripped to pieces. I'm going to have a level-ten freak-out right now. I don't know what happened. I had taken them out of the closet and hung them up on the rack while I finish the rest of the collection. I left to go to lunch with Amanda and Ashley, and when I returned, they were in pieces all over the floor. I needed those dresses. They are the main pieces to my collection. I don't know what to do. There isn't enough time to make the dresses over again."

Mia sounded on the verge of tears as she recounted what had happened. Sadie felt like her heart dropped to her feet. Who would do something like that? "Did you show anyone the dresses besides me?

"No. You were the first person outside my family I have shown anything to. I haven't even shared this with Ashley and Amanda, and they're my best friends."

"I'm so sorry, Mia. Maybe we can redo them in time for the showcase?" She was hoping Mia would say yes, and they could fix the problem together. Instead, all she heard was uncomfortable silence on the other end of the phone, which only made her worry even more.

"No. It's impossible to redo them in time. I knew I shouldn't have gotten my hopes up. This is nothing but a sign that it's not meant to be, but thanks for trying. I'm just going to back out of the show while I can. I'll see you later."

Sadie had finally done something good to help someone, and it all was ruined. She must have the worst luck imaginable. What was she doing wrong? Was she being punished for ignoring her gift for so long?

"Hey, baby. You ready to go?"

She looked up at Jace as he stood in front of her. The only good thing going on in her life was Jace, but even that had a bad side attached to it, which she couldn't escape.

"Baby, is there something wrong?" he asked as he sat next to her.

She didn't want to confide in him about Mia. She was ashamed to think that way, she wasn't sure she could trust him. She used to tell Jace everything, but now she didn't trust him. It had a lot to do with Adam and all the secrets between the three of them. So she decided not to say anything about Mia and the dresses.

"Nothing. I was just thinking about everything is all," she said, fake smiling the best she could in the moment.

Jace looked as if he were studying her face and could tell she was lying, but instead of pushing the issue, he gave her a quick kiss on the lips and held out his hand to her. "Then let's go surfing."

She smiled and took his hand. "Yeah. I can't wait to get out there on the waves."

★★★★★

Sunset Cliffs had always been Sadie's favorite surf spot, and the view was breathtaking. She'd known how to surf ever since she was a little girl thanks to her mom, who had been a badass on the water. She'd taught both Sadie and Laura how to surf when they were still young. When Jace came into Sadie's life, she took it upon herself to teach him, and he had no objections whatsoever. In fact, he was a pretty good surfer for someone who had just learned a few years back. He had always been willing to do anything she wanted to do.

When Sadie and Jace got all settled in a perfect spot,

she pulled her top over her shoulders, revealing her teal bikini top that wrapped around her ribs and tied in the back. Then she slid down her shorts to uncover her matching bottoms with small oval cutouts by her hips. As she was putting her clothes in her bag, she felt a warm hand on her hip. She leaned back and felt Jace turn her head gently as he locked his lips on hers.

He broke the kiss and looked at her. "I'm ready to go surfing now," he said chuckling.

Unfortunately, she might need a minute to recover. Her legs felt like jelly, and her belly was doing somersaults. She leaned up and gave Jace one more quick kiss on the lips before finally heading to her board. The ocean was calling to her.

★★★★★

Sadie was lying on her board floating with the current. Her mind was running over everything. She knew she had to be missing something. Why was everything falling apart? She wanted to help people, and it wasn't just because of her mother. It had become more than that. Sadie generally loved watching people being happy around her. Even when she'd become shy and sad after the death of her parents and didn't want to talk to people because of the pain, she still loved to see people being happy around her. A part of her wanted to be happy with them or even be the reason behind it.

So what's the issue now? she silently wondered as she closed her eyes. *How am I failing so badly?*

Why do select people get help and others don't?

Why is Amy different from my aunt?

If I could take away my mother's pain, I would.

Sadie shot up on her board as something clicked into place. How could she have been so stupid? It was right in front of her face the whole time.

She quickly paddled to the shore. She left her board on the shore and swiftly walked up to Jace. There was something she had to ask as soon as possible

"Hey, baby. You ready to go?" he asked her.

"No. I need to ask you something, and I want the truth no matter how ugly it may be. Okay?"

He was extremely quiet and looked at her intensely before finally nodding in agreement.

She took a breath of relief. "What did you mean when you said you were protecting me from your family? And how are you different from them?"

Jace pinched his brows together and swallow before finally speaking. "My mother wants revenge. She blames everyone and wants everyone to know her pain."

"What does that mean exactly?"

"It means she will stop someone like you from helping someone for the better because she doesn't believe it's fair for them to get a happy ending when my aunt never got the chance."

Sadie felt her blood begin boiling. She suddenly knew the truth. "Does Adam believe in everything your mother does?"

"My brother always took my mother's pain more personally than anyone. He hated seeing her hurt and would try anything to erase it. So if that means carrying out my mother's wishes no matter what, he would do it."

"You don't want the same thing?" she asked.

"No, I don't,"

"Why? She is your mother, and that's your family. What is so important to turn against that? I mean, befriending me and finding out who my mother was would be the perfect opportunity to hurt me, so I can feel the pain your mother feels every day." She really needed to know if she could trust him once and for all.

"Simple. It's because of you"

"What does that mean?"

"When I was younger, I was like Adam. It hurt me to see my mother's pain and even now, I still care about my mother. I'm sure you would feel the same way if you were in my shoes. I used to think that if I was good enough and did everything I could to make her happy and bring a smile to her face, then she would forget about her pain and enjoy the life she had with Dad, Adam, and me. However, it never worked. The pain always came back in my mother's eyes, and she was sad all over again. Then one day I met a sweet girl and saw how pure and beautiful she was and how she cared about everything and everyone around her.

"I watched how you always made sure your big sister was happy and how your relationship with Luke grew from being strangers to having an unbreakable bond as older brother and younger sister. Do you get what I'm saying, Sadie? You're a beautiful angel, and because you exist, things are not as bad as my mother made them out to be. I know you are worth fighting for."

She had no words. She really wanted everything he'd said to be true because she loved him so much. She had the power to see if he was telling the truth, but she didn't want to cross that line. She feared it would become her fallback to check and see if someone was lying to her always.

She was just going to have to trust that what he was telling her was the truth. Besides, she had something even more important to do and that was to convince Mia that she could redo those dresses in time for the showcase. She might even call Ashley and tell her everything and see if she would want to help. She wished she could even call Amy and see if she wanted to come out and make some new friends. Ashley and the girls would probably like Amy if they got to know her; plus, Amy could see what a cool girl she really was. But with the current situation, introductions would have to wait for another time. Sadie didn't want to get ahead of herself, so she would address one problem at a time. She knew what she was up against now so she will have to confront Adam as well.

★★★★★

Mia opened the door with a complete and utter look of defeat on her face. It was sad to witness, and it only made Sadie's anger toward Adam grow even hotter. He'd tried to ruin Mia's dream for no reason at all.

"Hey, Sadie. What are you doing here?" Mia questioned.

"I'm here to help you redo the dresses for the showcase."

"I already told you that it's impossible for me to redo them in time. The best thing I can do is pull out now before I embarrass myself in front of all those people."

"I'm sorry, but that is not the right kind of attitude

to have. You are a better person than to let one setback derail you from your dream. You have real talent that those judges need to see. Please don't give up now. You are almost there." She hoped her words were sinking in a little.

"I don't want to quit, but you don't know the amount of work it takes to make one dress. You are talking about two dresses in four days on top of finishing everything else for the showcase."

"Well, it's a good thing you're not alone then, isn't it?"

She couldn't help but smile as she saw Ashley and Lisa come around the corner. She caught the stunned look on Mia's face when she saw them as well.

"Hey, guys. What are you doing here?" Mia asked nervously.

"Sadie called us, and all I have to say is this: Come on, girl. With the four of us, we can get this done, and then you will totally kick ass at that showcase," Ashley said.

"No excuses, Mia. We are staying no matter how long it takes because that what friends are for," Lisa added.

Sadie looked back at Mia again and was pleased to see that the look of defeat was gone. They were finally making progress. Mia had to know now that her friends weren't going to let her just give up. Together, they could overcome anything, and that was what true friendship was about. Sadie knew she was right when she saw Mia step aside to let them all inside so they could get right to work.

★★★★★

"I'll tell you one thing," Ashley said. "I will never take

for granted the clothes I buy at the mall after today. Who knew making a dress was so hard? All fashion designers get an A-plus from me. It is a tough act to follow." She said as she leaned back against the bed with her third piece of pizza in her hand.

Mia laughed. "Thanks a lot. But honestly, I wouldn't have been able to pull this off without you guys. You all totally rock."

Sadie smiled even though she was completely exhausted. Ashley wasn't kidding when she said making clothes was hard work. They had started at ten o'clock that morning, and it was now nearing midnight. Lisa had volunteered to go get food in the last hour, afraid that everyone would pass out from hunger. She came back with every girl's best friend: two extra-large pepperoni pizzas and a two-liter of soda.

The newly redone dresses hung on the wall, and they looked amazing, especially considering three girls with no experience had helped put them together in a single day. Sadie couldn't help but winced a little when she accidentally squeezed her fingers. She'd poked her fingers more than a couple of times with a needle, but she honestly didn't mind as long as the dresses were completed. Now that they were done, Mia was officially all set for the showcase.

"So, Mia, do you feel better now? You ready to show those judges what you are made of?" Ashley asked.

Sadie was relieved when she saw the happy look on Mia's face. It was like a complete night-and-day switch from when they'd first arrived. Darkness and clouds had been covering her face. Now Mia's face looked like the sun was shining down on her.

"I do feel a lot better, and it's all thanks to my awesome friends."

"That is excellent to hear, but I'm calling it a day for two reasons. One, I'm tired, and two, I need to get up early for my class," Ashley noted. "You ready to go, Lisa?"

"Yeah, I'll see you later girls."

Once Ashley and Lisa left, Sadie knew it was time for her to call it a night as well. "Did you need help with the cleanup?" she asked Mia.

"No, I'm good. I still have a ton of energy to burn through, but thanks for the offer. You go on and head home."

"Okay," Sadie said. "If you're sure, then I'll see you later."

"Hey, Sadie," Mia called after her.

"Yeah?"

"Thank you."

Sadie smiled. "Sure thing. Good night."

★★★★★

When she opened the front door, everything was off except the lamp in the living room. It was after midnight when she finally got home, Jace was probably already asleep. Sadie was a bit disappointed because she had missed him. He'd sent her a couple of texts throughout the day to check on her, which was nice.

She assumed he was probably trying to give her the respect to handle her own life the way she wanted, but now she wanted to see him more. She took her shoes off at the front door, put her stuff on the couch, and quietly made her way to Jace's room. She found him asleep on the bed with his right hand flat on his stomach and his left arm at his side. She went to the dresser to grab one of his shirts and quickly changed before crawling into bed. As she leaned down and placed a light kiss on his neck and watched him slowly stir awake. When Jace finally opened his eyes and smiled, he pulled her into his embrace. She made herself comfortable and rested her head on the left side of his chest as she wrapped her right arm around his stomach.

"Hey, baby. I missed you today. Did everything go well?" Jace asked sleepily.

"Yeah. I couldn't be happier," she said while snuggling closer into his embrace.

Jace lightly kissed her on the top of her head and pulled her closer in before settling back into sleep.

★★★★★

Java chip frappes were so tasty. Chocolate had always been Sadie's weakness, and after a long run on the beach, it was a perfect treat. She took off her shoes and made her way back to the beach so she could walk along the water with her cold drink in hand. As she made her way toward the water, she bumped into the one person she didn't expect to see.

"Hey, Amy," Sadie said. "How have you been?"

"Why are you asking? Shouldn't you already know because of that mysterious gift that you have?"

She flinched hearing her snide tone. Amy was obviously still mad at her. She could read that loud and clear without her gift. Enough was enough. It was time to prove the truth to Amy once and for all.

"I'll tell you what, You put one particular thought in your mind, anything you want—and if I am right, then can you drop the snide attitude toward me and just accept what I tell you as the truth."

"Okay, let me think … Oh wait. How about instead I just tell you the same answer I told you before, and that is no. Now leave me alone."

"Why are you being this way to me?" Sadie asked. "All I wanted to do was help you and become your friend. You don't deserve the situation you are in, and I want to help you get out of it."

"You lied to me from the beginning, so there is no way to know if you're telling me the truth. But there one major issue that I have with you, and that is *magic is not real!*"

"It's not magic," Sadie said. "I can't really explain it myself, but I know that it is something my mom protected and used to help as many people as she could. And so I will do the same because I am her daughter and I truly want to help."

"Okay, I'll humor you for a bit. I'll ask the one question you still haven't given me an answer to," Amy said. "Why do you want to help with someone's life problems when it doesn't concern you and is none of your business?"

That was the one question she was still asking herself from time to time, and now she was supposed to answer it honestly to someone she was trying to make believe in her and her abilities. She could kick herself for sticking her foot in her mouth yet again.

"No answer again," Amy said. "You act like you have all the answers and are this saint, but in truth, you don't know what you're doing. I told you about my father being a firefighter—a true hero who helped people. And you know what? He had an answer for helping people. He used to tell me that it was his role in life to help people because he saved one life and that life could save more lives in the future, and so on. So how about we go about our day now since I have made my point? You have already taken enough of my time for this useless conversation." Amy was gone.

When will I learn? Sadie thought.

She needed to watch what she said and be able to back it up. She couldn't think of anything to say, so instead of making things worse, she turned and headed to the beach for her long walk home, hoping it would give her time to think.

CHAPTER 16

FOUR DAYS HAD PASSED SINCE Sadie had run into Amy at the coffeehouse, and the encounter hadn't left her mind once. She still didn't know how to go about fixing things but didn't want to give up. It was the day of Mia's showcase, and Sadie needed to get ready to support her friend.

It was impressive to see the huge amount of confidence inside Mia now. She couldn't wait to see her whole collection live and show the judges how talented she was.

"Wow, babe," Jace said. "You look beautiful."

She smiled, looking at Jace from the bathroom mirror. "Thanks," she said while applying her mascara. She had decided on a royal-blue dress that tied around her neck and exposed her back. It ended just above her knee and flared out just a little to give her a slim hourglass figure, which she loved. She finished it off with a pair of silver open-toed, one-inch heels. Since she didn't like to go to high when it came to heels, because she was already five seven without them and finally she curled her hair and went with simple makeup that brought out her features to finish the look.

Jace's hand grabbed her hair and guided it all off her left shoulder so he could place a kiss on her bare skin. He placed another on her neck. She had a feeling she knew where this was going.

"You're going to ruin my hard work if you keep this up, babe." Her argument wasn't even convincing herself, as she was leaning into Jace and tilting her head for him. A girl has only so much willpower. When she felt his hand on her stomach, those familiar butterflies started flying in her belly.

"Sorry, but I need a taste," he told her. "You look too appealing for me not to do this."

Jace tilted her head to the right and sealed his mouth over hers. She felt him lick her lower lip, so she opened his mouth and deepened the kiss.

Jace's hand travel up her left arm, past her shoulder, and all the way to the back of her neck where her dress was tied and pull the knot as her dress fell at a puddle at her feet.

"We shouldn't do this," she said. "Ashley will be here soon."

"I think we should," Jace said with a smile

She wasn't wearing a bra since there was no need with her choice of dress. He lightly traced each of her nipples before pinching them with his first finger and thumb and then gently tugging them. She couldn't help but moan in pleasure. It felt so good, and it was making her feel very needy.

Jace guided her by her hips to the bed and told her to

bend over. She could feel the air-conditioning against her hot skin as he pulled her panties down.

He thrust into her, and it felt delicious to her. The pleasure was already starting to build in her when he started a steady rhythm. She begin to squirm as she knew her orgasm was fast approaching.

"Let go, baby. I've got you," Jace whispered as he wrapped his arm around her stomach and started to pound into her.

She shattered into pieces at that moment, and Jace followed closely behind by burying his face into her neck.

She held herself up with the last of her strength Even though she was tired and all her limbs felt like jelly, and she probably had to fix her hair and makeup and straighten out her dress, it still was worth it. And she'd do it all over again if she could.

Jace kissed her on the shoulder and then pulled out of her while pulling her up and turning her to face him. He placed a deep kiss on her lips.

"You are so warm and soft," he said. "And you smell like warm honey and milk."

"Thanks," She said with a laugh. "Now get out of here, so I can get ready by the time Ashley gets here."

When she looked up, she saw Jace smile at her before turning and leaving her be. She honestly was glad about that because she wasn't sure her legs could handle another round even if she did want to.

★★★★★

She had never been to a fashion showcase, so she couldn't help but take everything in as she walk in. There were white folding chairs in rows down both sides of the runway. The runway itself looked like eight large marble blocks in a row and stood about six inches off the floor. There was a black backdrop with large white paper daisies placed sporadically on it. She assumed the black-and-white color scheme was to draw out the colors of the students' collections.

Ashley, Amanda, Lisa, Erica and Sadie grabbed some seats in the middle row. As she looked over the pamphlet she had grabbed at the door, she saw there would be five collections being shown by five different students. According to what Mia had told her, the winner would received an internship to work under a famous designer for a year. It would be an incredible opportunity to gain experience and knowledge, all with the hope of being able to open their own line in the future.

"Wow. I'm nervous, and it's not even my collection," Lisa said with a smile.

"Well we did help with two dresses," Ashley noted. "I'm feeling the pressure myself, and if any of these people say anything bad about Mia's collection, I might kick their butts."

Sadie couldn't help but laugh. "Can you imagine how Mia must feel right now? We only helped a little, but she designed the whole collection from scratch."

"Yeah, you're probably right. I wouldn't be surprised if she was a ball of nerves in back," Erica said.

"Yeah, I hear you," Ashley added.

"I'm going to go check on her. I'll be right back," Sadie said as she left her bag on the chair and slid down the row toward the back door.

The location for the showcase was an old fashion warehouse. It was actually kind of cool seeing the design and all the original wood. The ceiling was exposed, leaving all the piping and wiring visible, which made it even better.

She went through the back door behind the backdrop, which led to another big room filled with models. Some were talking to each other, while others were getting last-minute alterations to the outfits they were wearing. Sadie did have to admit all the clothing she saw was outstanding. She was amazed that all these designs had come from a sinple idea, then been sketched out, and made real.

After looking around, Sadie finally found Mia in the back of the room looking at her sketchbook.

"Hey, how are you?" Sadie asked when she reached her.

Mia looked at her, and Sadie saw a mix of fear, excitement, and confidence in her expression. "I'm okay or should I say about okay as I can be since I feel like I'm going to throw up at the moment," Mia said with a nervous laugh.

"You have nothing to worry about. I know you'll be great. Those judges will be so impressed by what you have pulled together."

"I wish I had your unwavering confidence right now," Mia admitted.

"Believe in yourself, and other people will believe in you as well. I'll let you finish getting ready. Ashley and the girls and I will be in the crowd cheering you on."

"I know I told you this before, but I really owe you

a big thank-you. Without you, I really doubt I would be here."

"I had nothing to do with you being here," Sadie said. "Your talent brought you here, and you should be proud. All I did was give you a little push. Good luck. I'll see you after the show."

"I don't know about that. You seem like my own personal guardian angel, and I'm grateful for it."

Sadie had no words, so she just smiled and headed back to her seat. It was touching to hear Mia say that, but she hadn't done anything different than what any friend would have done.

"Well, I bet you must feel like you're walking on cloud nine after working so hard to get your friend here. Don't you?"

She frowned but wasn't surprised anymore to hear Adam's voice. It was starting to become an annoying pattern. "What do you want?"

"Now that isn't a very friendly tone. I thought we were friends."

"Friends don't do mean things to other friends."

"Mean things? I don't believe I have done anything mean to you, as you say. How about you refresh my mind about these mean things I have done?"

"Come on, Adam. I know the truth, You have been going out of your way to hurt the people I have been trying to help. First Jenny losing her internship all of sudden after you found us studying together, and now Mia's dresses being ruined right before her big showcase."

"Wow. That is impressive, Do you have any proof that I did any of that?"

"Well, no. Jace told me everything about your mom. Of course you will honor your mom's wishes."

"Those are some strong accusations, my dear, but you are missing the big picture, I think."

"What is the big picture that I'm missing?" Sadie asked.

"That what you are doing is wrong," Adam noted. "You shouldn't mess with certain people's lives and not others. We should all have an equal chance to follow our fate and face whatever consequences that comes from that."

"But didn't your mother say that people with gifts have a responsibility to help people who don't?"

"Yeah, she said that. And who helped my aunt? It sure wasn't your mother. And so, in turn, everybody should be equal across the board, and I'm going to make sure that happens. It's only fair, and no matter how you apologize for your mother's actions, it won't change my mind."

"Then why try to be my friend and be so nice to me at first? Was it just a sick joke you were playing on me?"

"You are beautiful, and I want you to be mine," Adam told her.

She felt like she suck in a gulp of air. *Why would he say something like that?*

"My baby brother isn't the only one to fall in love," Adam continued. "It's just unfortunate you're the daughter of such a selfish woman. I was hoping that I could talk some sense into you so you could be different from that lady and learn from her past mistakes or else."

"What are you talking about?" Sadie asked.

"Stop messing with things that you shouldn't be

involved with, Sadie. This is the last warning I'm going to give you."

She just looked at Adam and felt his hand on her cheek before he turned around and walked away from her. Sadie kept telling herself she wasn't afraid, because she was doing the right thing, and that's what mattered. Still, she wondered what Adam was talking about.

"There you are. The show is about to start." Ashley said

"Yeah, you're right, Let's get to our seats before Mia's collection comes out." As she absently made her way back to her seat with a mind adrift, hoping Ashley was following.

"Sadie, are you okay?" Ashley questioned.

"Yeah, no worries," she whisper

They didn't have time for this. It was Mia's moment to shine. She put all her worry and stress to the back of her mind and took her seat to cheer on her friend.

★★★★★

The show was great. Sadie was honestly impressed by everyone who participated. There had been a lot of amazing designs. The judges are going to have a hard time deciding the winner.

Mia told her friends that the winner wouldn't be announced. Instead, the judges would send letters to each of the designers in about a week to let them know the results. So after Mia packed up her clothes, they all went out for a late lunch to celebrate Mia's first showcase and the many more they were sure would follow in the future.

★★★★★

As Sadie made dinner late that night, she was pleased to say it had been a good day with the girls. Besides the one minor setback of Adam showing up.

"Jace, I have something to tell you."

"What's up?" he asked while he finished cutting up the celery.

She paused for a moment because she knew this was going to kill the mood, but he had to know.

"I saw Adam today."

Jace put down the knife down and turned toward her. "Weren't you at Mia's showcase today with Ashley and the girls?"

She nodded at him and then waited for the question that was on the tip of his tongue.

"What was Adam doing there then? What did he want?" Jace questioned.

"Me," she said quietly.

CHAPTER 17

"WHAT DO YOU MEAN HE was there for *you*?" Jace asked as he walked over to her.

"He came to me when I was alone in the hallway after talking with Mia and pretty much told me to stop using my gift to mess with people's lives. Those were his words."

"That asshole just won't stop. You don't deserve this," he said. "I'll deal with him right now." She could see the anger in Jace's eyes. He was trying to protect her.

She came up and placed her hand on the side of his neck. "No. Please don't. I didn't tell you about Adam so you can fix the situation. I need to do this on my own, and that means whatever happens, I'll handle it. I need you to trust me."

"You shouldn't have to deal with this. He's my brother, and my family is causing you problems that you don't need in your life."

"It's okay. It's not your fault, and in truth, I get where your brother is coming from. My mom did fail to save your aunt, and I'm sorry about that. But I'm not going to fail no matter what," she said. "I will show Adam and anybody else that I'm here, and I will do what I can to help as many people as I can."

"How are you so strong, baby?" Jace asked as he pulled her into a hug and kissed the top of her head.

"I'm not strong. I'm about as weak as the next person, but I'm learning about my own strength, and I'm trying to be as strong as I can," she said while cuddling in closer to his chest.

"I love you, baby," Jace said, giving her a squeeze.

"I love you too."

"Okay, now that that is out of the way, let's grab a bite to eat," Sadie suggested. "I'm hungry." She laughed as she got started browning the hamburger meat in the pan.

"I'm hungry too but for something else entirely," Jace said as he leaned in and lightly kissed the side of her neck.

She smiled as she put the spatula down on the counter and turned around. She kissed Jace deeply on the lips and then lightly pushed him away. The look of shock on his face was laughable. He obviously wanted to continue what he had started and was shocked that she didn't.

"Down, boy," she told him. "I do enjoy what you're thinking, but I need food, especially with the workout you keep putting me through."

Jace smiled at her. "Okay, you win. We will eat."

She laughed and looked over her shoulder at Jace. "Besides, you love my tacos. I'm the taco grill master in this house."

"You got that right, babe," he said, laughing as he walked over to the fridge.

★★★★★

The last thing Sadie remembered was lying on the bed on her stomach with her laptop open while she worked on her book. She was comfortable and relaxed and began dozing off. There was just one thing she couldn't get over. She had the distinct feeling that someone was watching her. Maybe it was Jace. When she'd left him to go to her room, he was watching a ball game.

She smiled when she felt his touch on her cheek, thinking he was there to come get her and carry her to his room, where they could finish what he'd started earlier. A warm fire began traveling through her body as Jace's touch went from her cheek to down her shoulder.

She started to squirm as she turned her head up, hoping Jace would finally kiss her. When his lips met hers, the small fire that had been stirring in her belly turned to a strong blaze that took over her whole body. She had to open her eyes because suddenly it felt like she couldn't get enough air. She began to wrap her arms around Jace's neck but froze when she realized that it wasn't Jace kissing her.

Sadie tore her mouth away and scrambled off the bed as quickly as she could before running to the corner of the room.

"Adam, what are you doing here?" she whispered as she went and shut her door quietly, hoping that Jace wouldn't hear.

Adam smiled and walked over to her. "What does it look like I'm here for?"

Sadie froze where she stood. Why couldn't she make herself move away from him? What was wrong with her?

"Why are you here, and why do you keep doing this? You know I'm with Jace, so you need to stop doing this. Besides, Amy is your girlfriend."

"You still want to fight your destiny? You know deep down that you are meant to be with me, I can feel your heart pound when I'm around you."

Sadie swallowed as she felt him place his hand over her heart. She wanted to grind her teeth to dust because he was right. She did feel something for him, and no matter how many times she told herself she loved Jace and he was the one for her, she couldn't hide the truth from her body. It betrayed her every time.

"So what if you might be right?" she said. "I can't be with you for several reasons. My biggest reason hearing your views about people and my mother. I have begun to hate you after hearing those words."

Adam smiled at her and then leaned down, placing his lips on hers and pressing her against the door as he opened her mouth to deepen the kiss. She grabbed a handful of Adam's shirt, and instead of pushing him away like her brain told her to, she pulled him closer.

When Adam broke the kiss, he smiled and looked down at Sadie.

"Are you sure you're with Jace? I think you're trying to run from the truth. My brother may have found you first, but you are meant to be with me. And as far as your special ability, you will learn soon enough that you shouldn't use it. And do you want to know how I know that? It's because I will make you stop."

"You can't make me stop," she told him. "This is what I want and what my mother wants for me as well."

"You have two choices, Sadie. You need to realize you're wrong and accept that your mom caused all this pain and suffering by her own selfish choices, and if you don't something terrible will happen that will open your eyes for sure."

"What do you mean something terrible will happen?" she asked.

"Exactly what it sounds like," he told her. "It's your choice, Sadie. You decide what the future holds. I am going to leave you with this, though. Did you ever wonder how I knew everything that you have been doing lately? Are you sure you have your trust in the right person? Are you sure what you think you know is actually the truth?"